S0-DXO-933

DATE DUE			

FIC
DIG

Diggs, Lucy.

Moon in the water.

M-S. -89-709

DISCARD

GODLEY MIDDLE SCHOOL LIBRARY
GODLEY, TEXAS 76044

790762   04123B

MOON
IN THE
WATER

GODLEY MIDDLE SCHOOL LIBRARY

MOON
·· IN THE ··
WATER

Lucy Diggs

GODLEY MIDDLE SCHOOL LIBRARY

■■■

ATHENEUM
1988
NEW YORK

Haiku in Chapter 3 quoted with permission Hokoseido Press, Tokyo.

Author: Fritz Rotter and M. Rotha; Title: "That's All I Want From You"; Publisher: Weiss and Barry; Date of original publication: October 21, 1954.

"Let the Good Times Roll" by Leonard Lee. © *1956 Atlantic Music Corp.* © *renewed 1984 and assigned to Atlantic Music Corp. Used by permission.*

"Earth Angel" by Dootsie Williams. Copyright 1954 by Dootsie Williams Publications. Copyright renewal 1982 by Dootsie Williams Publications. International copyright secured. All rights reserved.

"Summertime" by Dubose Heyward and George Gershwin. Copyright © *1935 by Chappell and Co., Inc. Copyright renewed. International copyright secured. All rights reserved. Used by permission.*

"Shall We Dance" by Richard Rogers and Oscar Hammerstein II. Copyright © *1951 by Richard Rogers and Oscar Hammerstein. Copyright renewed and assigned by Chappell and Co., Inc. International copyright secured. All rights reserved. Used by permission.*

Copyright © 1988 by Lucy Diggs

All rights reserved. No part of this book may be reproduced or transmitted in any form or by any means, electronic or mechanical, including photocopying, recording, or by any information storage and retrieval system, without permission in writing from the publisher.

Atheneum
Macmillan Publishing Company
866 Third Avenue, New York, NY 10022
Collier Macmillan Canada, Inc.
First Edition
Printed in U.S.A.

10 9 8 7 6 5 4 3 2 1

Library of Congress Cataloging-in-Publication Data

Diggs, Lucy.
Moon in the water.

Summary: A teenaged boy in the mid-1950s enters his horse in jumping events at horse shows in central California and fights with his abusive father, who wants him to help swindle customers at cock fights.
[1. Horses—Fiction. 2. Horse shows—Fiction.
3. Fathers and sons—Fiction] I. Title.
PZ7.D5765Mo 1988   [Fic]   87–19310
ISBN 0–689–31337–3

For Joan Vincent Cupples,
who believed from the beginning,
with gratitude and love

ACKNOWLEDGMENTS:

I should like to thank the following people for their encouragement and enthusiasm: my parents, James and Virginia Diggs, Hella Fluss, Beth Snortum, and Betty Hodson; the members of the Saturday Group, steadfast and astute as always: Joan Vincent Cupples, Caroline Fairless, Mary Rose Hayes, Patrick Jamieson, Kermit Sheets, Elizabeth Stewart, Katie Supinski, Marilyn Wallace. David Tresan and William Bridges provided valuable insights and information. I should also like to thank the riders at Chalk Hill Ranch and our trainers: John and Elizabeth Charlebois and Betty Kilham. And most especially, Shadow Catcher, a pinto like Blue who proved his worth in the show ring.

MOON
IN THE
WATER

1

■ ■ ■

JoBob had a secret, all his own, not like some of those where five or ten other people know it too, so it isn't really a secret at all. This one was *real*. Trumaine didn't know about it and they'd been buddies since kindergarten. Neither did Slim, and Slim managed the barn where JoBob worked every afternoon. JoBob's parents didn't know about it either. His parents didn't know spit.

The secret was always with him, somewhere in the back of his mind, but late in the afternoon when he'd finished riding, while he was doing his chores at the barn, it came bubbling up from the back of his mind right to the front. At five-thirty, Trumaine and K.T. went home for supper. Their mothers required them to be home for supper at six, but JoBob's mother didn't care when he came home. Half the time she wasn't even there. She'd be working late at her job at the telephone company, or in town at a church meeting.

So after K.T. and Trumaine and the other customers had left, JoBob walked around with Slim, helping him with the evening rounds. They looked into each stall, making sure that each horse was blanketed and comfortable. Then Slim locked the tack room and shut the barn doors. Sometimes Slim sat down on the bench in front of the barn. He'd drape his arms over the bench back and then he'd start to talk. He'd tell JoBob stories about the old days when he was a kid back in Texas. Or he'd talk about a horse's conformation—how you could get a sense of whether a horse had any jump in him by the way his bones were put together. Or he'd tell him horse trading stories, most of which ended up with Slim getting the better of somebody or another. But occasionally he'd tell stories on himself, too. Those evening times, when he was alone with Slim, were the second-best parts of JoBob's day. The best part came when Slim left; that's when the secret started.

JoBob was careful. When he walked out the front door of the barn with Slim, he picked up his book satchel and headed for the pasture behind the barn. That was the back way to his house—through the pasture, and then down the path through the woods that began where the pasture ended. He didn't wait for Slim to get in his truck and go on down the road to the highway. He made sure that Slim saw him heading for home. JoBob walked straight through the pasture, then edged into the woods where he lowered his book satchel to the ground and waited. Sometimes he waited a long time, sometimes a short time. He didn't know why. Different days needed different times.

4

But now it was October and the days were getting shorter, so JoBob's waiting time was getting shorter too, because he needed at least a little bit of daylight.

The wind gusted up the valley and rattled the leaves on the trees. JoBob turned up the collar of his jacket and listened. The sun was lowering down in the west and it seemed to be taking a lot of the daytime noises along with it. The sounds of the cars out on Route 99 petered out to soft swishes, and the birds started warming up for the evening concert. "Bobwhite, bobwhite?" called the quails. "Oo-hoo, oo-hoo," cooed the doves. Other birds that JoBob couldn't identify trilled and twittered. He couldn't figure out if the birds slept all day, or if he couldn't hear them because of all the other noises making paths in the air like the vapor trails of the big new jets coming into Moffitt Air Field. "Oo-hoo," he called. He sat still, waiting for an answer, and soon it came: "Oo-hoo, hoo-hoo-oo?" The dove's answer sent a shiver down his spine. It was time.

He went back down the road through the pasture and into the barn again, the shiver of anticipation getting stronger. Inside the barn the thick, yeasty smell of manure mingled with the grassy smell of hay and the pungent smell of horse. The horses made soft chewing noises while they worked on their hay, and an occasional whuffle or stomp. JoBob didn't turn on the lights. Someone might see them and that would blow the whole thing. Lights were for sissies anyway, and he could see in the dark as well as a cat.

He walked through the barn pretending that he owned Samantha and Charlie. They were the two best horses in the barn, and if they were his . . . He picked up a bucket and stopped at the oat bin to fill it up. Then he took a halter from a hook and went out back to the corral where Slim kept the lesson horses. And Blue.

Blue was JoBob's secret. JoBob rattled the bucket of oats and whistled low. Blue detached himself from the clump of big shadowy shapes and came trotting over, the big white blaze on his face looming bright in the gathering dusk. JoBob's heart jumped and he started talking to Blue as soon as he saw him. Blue understood everything JoBob told him. At least JoBob was pretty sure he did. At least he didn't give him any sass.

"That's the nicest thing about a horse," Slim would say, "beats a female to hell in a handbasket. My ex-wife was always yammering at me not to come in the house with my boots on. Wanting me to eat all sorts of weird food like eggplant and liver. Trying to make me do things I don't cotton to, like going to church." He'd stopped and spat. "Go to church on a Sunday when you could just as well be at a horse show, or out looking for a sale horse. Them A-rabs weren't so dumb. Kep' their horses in the tent right where they could be useful and let the women fend for themselves. Yessirree," he'd finished, clapping a hand on JoBob's knee. "Give me a horse any day."

"Yessirree," JoBob said now to Blue. "No sass from you, right?" Blue didn't answer right away. He stuck his nose in the bucket and started working on the oats while JoBob scratched the itchy place along the crest of his neck, under his mane.

6

Blue himself was no secret. Everyone at the barn knew he was there. He was noticeable enough with his one blue eye and wide white blaze, the big patches of white all over his coat, and his four white stockings. But everyone else thought he was just a lesson horse, good for nothing except trotting round and round the ring every afternoon, carrying beginners on his back while Slim yelled "up, down; up, down," teaching them how to post. Blue always got the beginners because he had such a good disposition. He never shied or kicked or bucked like some other horses did, and he trotted with a nice steady beat, which helped a beginner to get the rhythm.

No, Blue was no secret: What JoBob did with him was the secret. He'd been working all summer long, for almost six months now, training Blue, teaching him advanced movements on the flat and teaching him to jump.

"We're going to have fun today," JoBob told Blue. "And I mean *fun.*"

Blue raised his nose out of the bucket and looked at JoBob with both ears pricked forward. That meant he was alert and focused on the thing in front of him. "Something new for you," JoBob went on. "Couple of big jumps—oxers—about four feet six inches high. Think you can do it? Want to?" Blue lopped his ears back and lowered his head again to the bucket of oats.

"Okay," JoBob said, "I know you're hungry, but you can have the rest when we're done. It's not good for you to do too much work on a full stomach." He slipped the halter onto Blue's nose, took the lead shank in one hand and the bucket of oats in the other, and led Blue out the gate.

Outside the gate JoBob set down the bucket, took the halter off, and put the bridle on. "This afternoon I jumped Samantha through the combination we're going to do," JoBob said. "And if she can do it, I know you can. I never jumped anything that big before, and to tell you the truth, I was a teeny bit scared. But Sammie sailed right through it, and you know what? It was *fun!* And with you it'll be even more fun. So let's go. Time you stopped lollygagging around and started earning your keep." His voice squeaked and turned high like a girl's. Slim said that's what happened when you were fourteen and your voice was changing. Just couldn't tell when it would cut out on you. But JoBob knew it happened when he was upset. "I'm sorry, Blue," he said, "I know that's not fair. You do earn your keep trotting around with those beginners who hardly know how to post all afternoon, but this will set you free. There'll come a time when Slim'll know how good you are, and then you won't have to do that anymore."

JoBob looped the reins over Blue's neck, took two running steps and a jump, and he was on. He settled his seat into Blue's back and stretched his legs down along his sides. JoBob liked to ride him bareback, to be as close as he could, and to get the feel of him with nothing else in the way. Like the Indians rode. Blue cocked his ears back and pranced on all four legs. He knew what was up.

In the ring JoBob walked him around for a few minutes to make sure he was loosened up. Then he trotted and cantered, first to the left, then to the right. Blue put his nose down obediently and lengthened out his stride when JoBob asked him to. "Boy," he said, "if Slim could see you do that, he wouldn't call you crowbait anymore." Then he asked him to shorten his stride, and Blue did that too. He turned when JoBob asked him to, smooth and altogether, not with his front end first and his hind end dragging along later, the way he would with the girls in the lessons. Those girls had been told to use their legs to steer as well as their hands, but they couldn't ride well enough yet to do it.

Slim always said the horse ought to believe that God was at his mouth and the devil was at his belly. JoBob didn't like to ask stupid questions, so he'd thought about that for a long time. Finally he figured it out: the horse ought to trust you. He ought to know that you wouldn't jab him in the mouth, that your hands would be on the reins connected with the bit in his mouth in a sensitive, loving way. That was the God part. But if the horse slacked back, that's when you turned into the devil. Put your legs on him and made him move forward. Right away, at the exact moment you asked him to. And if he didn't, well, then you gave him what-for. Used your spurs, your crop. Let him know you meant business. JoBob's legs were strong because Slim was always giving him difficult horses to ride—young ones who didn't know better yet, or the ones like Samantha, whose owners let them get away with murder. They didn't try any funny stuff with JoBob, though. They knew better. So did Blue. At least now he did, because JoBob had taught him. He was the smartest, most willing horse JoBob had ever ridden. He just wished Slim knew that. But Slim had taken a dislike to Blue the first time he'd clapped eyes on him—last May when he'd come off the van from Colorado—and he hadn't changed his mind since.

They'd all been excited that day last May when the van was due in from Colorado. JoBob and Trumaine and K.T. hadn't even bothered to tease the girls on the school bus. They'd spent the whole time speculating about the horses Harold was sending out for Slim to sell.

"There'll be a black stallion, I bet," Trumaine said.

"Oh *sure*," K.T. said, "but maybe a nice Thoroughbred filly, leggy and big bodied, none of that waspwaisted stuff, so big and bold she'll be too good for a show horse. Slim'll send her to the track and she'll beat 'em all, win millions of dollars. . . ."

"Yeah, and we'll all go," JoBob said. "Sit in a box right along with the other owners. We'll wear gray fedoras and chomp big cigars just like them."

"Keep a stack of C-notes in our pockets," Trumaine put in, "from the money we made betting on her."

"That's right," K.T. grinned. "We'll call her California Queen, and she'll be a legend in her own time. . . ."

It wasn't every day six new horses arrived, and when the bus stopped on the highway by Gustavo's house they piled off and ran down the road to the barn, and didn't stop even then. They dumped their book satchels on the bench in front of the barn and ran

10

on to the corral out back. Nothing attracted people like a vanload of new horses, and there was already quite a crowd gathered along the corral fence. Besides Irma Goldstein and Mel Hackett, who were almost always there, there were some of the other customers, along with their friends and relations too.

Slim and Mel and Irma stood in a knot a few feet away from the others, their elbows folded on the top rail, one foot propped on the bottom one. Slim and Mel had known each other since they were kids back in Texas. Not only did they look alike—same squinty eyes and deep-tanned skin, gnarled hands and rolling gait—they sounded alike too. They'd been doing deals together since way back when too. Mel was a blacksmith, but a sale horse could get him out to the barn a lot quicker than a thrown shoe.

JoBob took one look at Slim's back and he knew that something was wrong.

"What the hell's gotten into Harold," Slim said, "sending me crowbait like this? He must still think we're cowboyin' back in Texas before the war. Hellfire, this is California and it's 1955. Times have changed, and people expect quality here. Right, Irma?"

Irma owned the barn and she liked to buy one or two green horses a year, bring them along, and sell them after they were going good. "Yes," she said. "I don't see a lot of quality in this bunch."

Slim grimaced. "Understatement of the year. There's something wrong with every damn one of them."

"That's a nice big rangy chestnut," Mel said, after awhile.

"But he's got a big ankle," Slim said. "And the bay mare's kind of cute, but she won't let anyone get near her. How the hell they got her on the van *I* don't know. And that ewe-necked black thing I wouldn't even have in my lesson string. . . ."

Slim and Mel and Irma kept talking while JoBob only half-listened. He was looking at the pinto in the corner, but it wasn't his unusual color or his one blue eye that caught JoBob's attention. It was the way he was standing all by himself, looking as if he didn't have a friend in the world.

"And that pinto takes the cake," Slim finished, looking really disgusted. "Harold said he was sending me some nice sale horses I could move out pretty quick." He paused and adjusted his hat, his eyes still on the horses in the corral. "Move out to the killer, maybe, but I don't have to send off to Colorado for dog food."

"Maybe they're doers," JoBob suggested. "Useful." Two of Slim's favorite concepts.

"Maybe," Slim replied, though he didn't sound convinced. "Well, might as well find out. You boys take your pick and we'll see what they can do."

JoBob got a halter and went to get the pinto in the corner. JoBob wanted him to feel better and he knew what it was like to be picked last. At school he was picked last for every team except baseball.

"JoBob," Slim said, "I'm surprised at you. Thought I'd taught you a little something about horseflesh."

"He looked lonely," JoBob said.

"Other horses don't take to an odd-colored horse," Slim said. Then, "Oh well, sooner's as good as later, I reckon."

Trumaine picked an ordinary-looking brown gelding and K.T. took the rangy chestnut with the big ankle. "Come on, Blue," JoBob whispered while he tacked him up. He'd already named him Blue Chip. It fit. Blue eyes were supposed to be bad luck, but blue chips were the best chips in poker and JoBob had a feeling about this horse. He was a strange color, but he didn't have a ewe neck or a big ankle. His legs were straight, he had a powerful-looking rear end, a good top line, and a nice slope to his shoulder. Slim had taught him that horses with conformations like that often made good jumpers. Why couldn't he see it?

All the Colorado horses were pretty rank, and green too, but after they'd ridden around the ring awhile Slim's mood started to improve, and by the end of the day he seemed almost pleased. He sat with Mel and Irma on the bench in front of the barn, assessing the new horses. JoBob and Trumaine and K.T. stood nearby, cleaning their tack.

"That chestnut's not bad," Slim said. "Got a little snap to his knees and a nice long stride. If that ankle don't blow up, I ought to be able to sell him for a field hunter, at least."

"Ankle'll do," said Mel, who knew as much about all the other parts of a horse as he did about feet. At least he talked like he did.

They went on like that about the other four, finding something good to say about each one. Finally, Irma said, "What about the pinto?"

"Make a lesson horse, maybe," Slim said. "He seems kind enough, and I'd get laughed off the street if I tried to sell him. What do you think?"

"It's okay with me," Irma said. "The way business is picking up we could use another lesson horse."

JoBob had been riding there at Oak Knoll Farm for nearly four years and he'd ridden a lot of horses. Up until then he'd never seen one that caught his fancy the way Blue did. So he was relieved that Blue wasn't going to be sold, but it made him sad to think that Slim had such a low opinion of him. Lesson horses had a pretty hard life. But JoBob had already put in his two bits worth about Blue, so he cleaned his tack and kept his mouth shut.

Slim and Mel were going on about how much they might be able to get for the Colorado horses and, when those two started talking deals, the atmosphere charged up around them like the air before a thunderstorm. They were both good horsemen, but when they started talking money, they might as well have been discussing loads of firewood. Like they didn't give two figs about the horse, just about how much money was going to go into their pockets. Or, and they seemed to like this even better, how much they could put over on the buyer—like the time Slim filed the teeth down on an old gelding and traded him even-up for a two year old. JoBob had said he didn't think that was honest, but Slim insisted that had nothing to do with horse trading. "It's economics, pure and simple. Honesty never bought no groceries." If someone was stupid enough to think a twelve-year-old was two or three, that was no skin off Slim's back. JoBob didn't like it when Slim talked like that. It reminded him too much of his father.

· · ·

14

The wind gusted leaves off the big oak tree in front of the barn, and JoBob sighed, thinking about Slim and the Colorado horses. He had sold them all over the summer, except for the ewe-necked black mare. And just last week he'd sold her. That mare was the ugliest horse JoBob had ever seen, but when Slim was in the mood he could sell a bikini to an Eskimo. Slim had been right about Blue, too. Sort of. He *was* a good lesson horse. But he was a lot more than that.

Blue tossed his head and nudged at the bit. "Okay, Blue," JoBob said. "The days are sure getting shorter and I know you'd like to jump while we can still see." Blue's answer was to break spontaneously into a canter as if he were already heading for a jump. JoBob smiled, then brought him to a halt on the long side of the ring where the triple combination was—a vertical, then three short strides to a big oxer, and one short stride to the last one. "See that, Blue? That's going to be your lesson for today. It'll teach you to shorten a little and jump round over the oxers. Want to try it?" Blue tossed his head, which JoBob took for agreement. JoBob jumped Blue back and forth over the crossrail at a trot, to warm up his jumping muscles. Then he cantered over a green and white striped vertical fence that was set at three feet six inches.

He practiced getting Blue to the base. Blue had such a long stride that he liked to take off long and jump flat over the fence. But JoBob wouldn't let him. He wanted him to curl over the jump, nice and round, like Charlie. Charlie was the best horse in the barn, was conformation hunter champion at just about every show he went to. Besides, the triple combination was set for a short stride. Blue wouldn't be able to jump it by lengthening out and powering through the way he wanted to, the way he would if JoBob let him.

JoBob collected him around the turn and headed for the line of three. Blue jumped so round over the first fence that JoBob got thrown forward, but Blue went right on through the line to the two big oxers and by the end JoBob was hanging on his neck. "Hoo-ee!" he yelled when they landed. Then, "Rats." The "hoo-ee" was for how good Blue was, and the "rats" was for how bad *he* was. He hadn't been jumped loose like that in a long time.

Blue squealed and bucked around the turn. JoBob laughed and patted him. "You ought to be proud of yourself," he said. "It was fun, wasn't it?"

Blue squealed again, and bucked playfully. He was having as much fun as JoBob was. JoBob crouched low onto Blue's neck and let him gallop. "Let's go," he whispered, "let's jump out of this old ring and take off! We can go on and on until, until . . ." He pulled Blue up. Until what? Where did he want to go? He didn't know. Just until they weren't here anymore. Well, maybe there was nothing wrong with right here, but when he left the barn and had to go home, that was a different story. "Oh well," he sighed. "I've got you. Let's jump that triple again. And this time I promise to stay with you."

He cantered a circle to get Blue paying attention again, jumped one fence to warm up, and then headed for the triple. They jumped into the first fence exactly

16

right—better than the last time. The next one was good too. Then JoBob felt Blue gather his hindquarters beneath him. He thrust off the ground and sailed over the last fence. It was as good a fence as Blue had ever jumped.

JoBob grinned and was about to give Blue a pat when a bright light hit him in the face, so bright he couldn't see. He blinked, trying to get the bright whirling spots out of his eyes. Lights from where? What was going on? Blue cantered on around the ring, waiting for JoBob to do something; but JoBob was frozen. Lightning? The police? His mind wasn't working any better than his eyes were.

"What in the Sam Hill is going on here?"

JoBob's ears were working all right. Well enough to identify the voice. Slim!

2

■■■

J oBob's heart stopped beating. The one thing he'd been afraid of. The one thing that would blow it all. Now Slim would kick him out of the barn, so JoBob might as well be dead. If he had to go home in the afternoons, if he had to hang around his house on Saturday and Sunday with no place else to go . . . "Please don't make me leave, Slim, I won't do it again. You didn't pay any attention to Blue, see, and I wanted to try him, find out what he could do, see if . . . if . . ."

Slim stood between his truck and the ring, backlit by the headlights of his truck. All JoBob could see was the dark outline of his shape.

"Slim? Please? I promise . . ." He set off again, all wound up, desperate to know what was going to happen. Then he heard something besides the words tumbling out of his own mouth.

A laugh. Slim was laughing.

"What's funny?" JoBob asked, utterly confused.

"Well, now, it's not exactly *funny*. Big surprise is more like it." Slim took off his hat and scratched his head. "Did I see what I think I did?"

"What do you think you saw?"

"I thought I saw you jumping this nag through that triple. Bareback."

"That's right."

Slim waved his hand in a gesture that could have meant weariness, disgust, dismissal, or—an invitation, and he finished it off with "Well?"

"Well what?"

"Go on. Do it again. Then I won't just think it, I'll know it."

JoBob gathered up the reins and squeezed Blue with his legs. Okay, Blue, he told him mentally, let's do it again, just like before. Make it really good, because this is important. It could mean your life. And mine.

He cantered a circle and headed for the triple, so worried he could hardly think. But Blue cantered right along. *He* didn't seem to be worried. He jumped the first fence of the triple, then cantered right on through, over the first oxer, and the second. They'd done it! The wind gusted dust in the ring, whipped tendrils of Blue's mane and JoBob's hair. Instead of whooping again, like he wanted to, JoBob cantered off along the rail and pulled up next to Slim. Slim pushed his hat back off his forehead. Back in the woods an owl hooted, making the skin on the back of JoBob's neck prickle. Why wasn't Slim saying anything? Had he been awful?

"I'll be damned," Slim said at last. "If I hadn't seen it, I wouldn't believe it."

19

"He jumps pretty good, huh?" JoBob was gradually getting the idea that Slim wasn't mad, that he might even be impressed.

"Yep," Slim said. "Why don't you do the whole course? The one you did on Samantha this afternoon."

JoBob gave Blue the Important Message again and told himself to be careful. It wasn't just he and Blue pottering around in the ring by themselves. Slim was watching. This time counted.

He cantered a circle, as if he were in the show ring, establishing the pace he would need for the course, then he started around, paying attention to every detail he could think of. He engineered the approach to each fence, made sure that he got there at exactly the right spot, he didn't let Blue get strong or flat, he made smooth turns and good lead changes. The jumps were the best part. Blue flowed over them, smooth as the wind rippling through a wheat field. JoBob wished he could see him from where Slim stood. He bet he looked wonderful. He *felt* wonderful, but you could see things sometimes you couldn't feel. That's why it was important to have a groundman. And he'd never had a groundman with Blue. Maybe he was dropping his shoulder or twisting or . . .

"I'm proud, son," Slim said, "real proud."

"Honest? You're not mad? I know I'm not supposed to jump by myself."

"You ought to be ashamed." Slim's voice was cool and flat, the way he sounded when he was really tickled about something. JoBob smiled.

"You go put that horse away," Slim said, "and then

come on back out here. I want to talk to you." The same flat tone. JoBob felt gleeful. It was going to be all right. He thought.

Inside the corral he dumped the rest of the oats on the ground and hoped that Blue would be able to salvage some of it from the other horses. Then he told Blue good night and went back around to the front of the barn.

"Hop in," Slim said. "This wind makes my bones ache."

JoBob got in the other side of the truck. Slim started the motor and let it idle, turning the heat up to high. JoBob sank into the seat, tired suddenly, relaxing into the warmth.

"Now I want you to tell me about this," Slim said. "How long you been up to these shenanigans?"

JoBob told him the whole thing—how he'd felt sorry for Blue because he was so skinny and the other horses ran him off from the hay piles and wouldn't let him eat. "So I started bringing him a bucket of oats in the evening, after everybody else went home. Pretty soon he got to know me. And one day I thought I'd try him, see if maybe he could jump. Because I knew he wanted to, I could *tell*."

"You were right," Slim said, "and I'm impressed. I didn't think much of that little horse."

"I know," JoBob said, "but he's a pretty good jumper, isn't he?"

"Damn right," Slim said. "Almost as good as Charlie. But he's still pretty silly looking." Then he fell silent. JoBob waited.

Finally Slim spoke again. "I'll make you a deal, okay?"

"Depends on the deal."

Slim chuckled, a kind of "hee, hee," that he saved up for times when he was really pleased. "You don't say much, but you learn while your mouth is shut, now don't you?"

JoBob ducked his head in acknowledgment.

"That's the best way. If you're blabbering off at the mouth you can't take in anything with your eyes or your ears. Or your brain either. I kinda suspected that about you, but . . ."

JoBob was getting embarrassed. "So what's the deal?"

"You've done a good job with that horse, so I was wondering if you'd like him."

"Sure I like him. I like him a lot."

"Like him to have. To be your horse."

JoBob didn't breathe. Had Slim really said that? When he first started hanging around the barn he'd dreamed about having a horse of his own. But then he found out how much it cost to buy a horse and how much it cost to keep one, and he knew he'd never be able to have one. So he let go of that idea— no sense in wanting something you couldn't have. It was one of the few good things his father ever told him. But, but, now, just now Slim had said that he could have Blue. Hadn't he?

"Honest and truly?"

"Honest and truly," Slim said. "Seems like you've earned him."

"But I don't have any money. I can't pay the board."

22

"Mucking out will pay for the board. And maybe a few extra chores. You can clean tack. Help Gustavo unload the feed truck. Ride a couple of extra horses for me."

JoBob couldn't believe it. "Riding count for work? Ride to pay for Blue?"

"Hell yes," Slim said. "You're getting to be a good little rider. You can help me out."

"But what about K.T.?"

"I got enough stock for the two of you and K.T. is finishing up high school this year anyway. Who knows what he'll do then? Any old how, it's time you started reaping some of what you've sowed."

JoBob didn't quite understand that. For someone who said he was allergic to church, Slim sure sounded like a preacher sometimes. What counted was what he *did* understand: Slim had said he could have Blue. His own horse, just like Trumaine and K.T.

"And I can keep him in the barn? He won't have to be a lesson horse anymore?"

"You can," Slim said. "I reckon he's earned a permanent vacation from all them beginners." He slipped the gearshift into reverse. "I'll take you home now. It's gettin' late and they'll be worrying about you."

"No, they won't. They don't ever worry about me. They don't hardly know where I am. Or care either."

Slim slanted him a funny look. "Well, if I had a boy like you, I'd sure as hell want to know where he was at." Then he mumbled something that JoBob didn't quite hear. "Valuable," maybe.

His house was only a quarter mile away by way of the path through the pasture and the woods, but it was almost a mile down the highway. Slim turned the radio back on and they rode along without talking. JoBob didn't want to talk anyway. He needed to think before he got home, and he was worried about what Slim would think when he saw his house. JoBob had been careful about that. Trumaine was the only person at the barn who had seen his house and he and Trumaine had been friends for so long that Trumaine had been to his house before JoBob knew it was anything to be ashamed of.

3
■■■

W HEN THE HEADLIGHTS of Slim's truck picked up the outline of JoBob's house along with the heaps of car doors, twisted fenders, overturned bathtubs, snarls of baling wire, and a jumble of other junk littered all over the front yard, JoBob had an idea. "You can stop here," he said, "and turn around there," pointing to the Kawabatas' driveway. "I'll walk the rest of the way." Slim was no snob, but JoBob had his pride and he didn't want him to come close enough to see the tar paper patches on the house or the missing boards on the front porch. The junk in the front yard you couldn't miss, and that was bad enough. His father was always collecting stuff. He said you never knew when something might be useful. The thing was he never did anything with it, just kept adding until the yard looked more like the county dump than a place where somebody *lived*.

"Okay," Slim said. "See you tomorrow."

"You bet," JoBob said. "Thanks a lot."

Slim gave him a thumbs-up sign. Then he turned around in the Kawabatas' driveway, beeped two short ones on the horn, and drove back out toward the highway. The wind whipped fronds from the eucalyptus trees along the road. Low clouds scudded across the moon. JoBob shivered and shoved his hands in his pockets.

In the Kawabatas' garden the tomatoes and peppers and eggplants had already been plowed under. Dry cornstalks rattled in the wind. Only the pumpkins and squashes still grew, their leaves almost black in the moonlight, the pumpkins round and luminous, sprawling randomly across a corner of the garden plot. Not even the Kawabatas' dedication to order and neatness could make them grow in rows. JoBob knelt and cupped his hands around one of the pumpkins. Its skin was smooth and cool to the touch and the earth smelled rich and loamy. JoBob thought about the thick fruit inside the pumpkin skin, and the seeds nestled inside the fruit—so full the skin might want to burst. Which was the way he felt too. He smoothed his hands along the pumpkin, not wanting to go inside yet.

He was used to being outside. He could alert his senses to where he could hear as well as an animal, identify sounds that belonged—like field mice and rabbits stirring in the weeds, the whir of an owl's wings as it plummeted down from tree to earth, where it seized a mouse in one swift motion, a single sharp squawk from the mouse, another flurry of wings as the owl returned to the tree with its prey—or the barely audible whir of bats flying low, more a faint movement in the air than a sound. JoBob was as much at home as any animal with these nocturnal comings and goings and, like them, he could tell when there was another presence nearby. He felt it now. He crouched lower beside the pumpkin, trying to identify it. He held his breath and listened hard. There it was! At the other end of the garden, near the house, a shape almost as still as his own, but nothing to be afraid of, something told him.

"Hello?" he called softly.

"Hello," came back. A girl's voice.

"That you, Mariko?"

"Yes. That you, JoBob?"

They both stood up. "What are you doing out here?" they asked at almost the same time.

"Jinx, you owe me a Coke," JoBob said.

"What?"

"Oh, it's just something you say when two people say the same thing at the same time."

"Well, what *are* you doing out here? It's cold."

"I know," JoBob said. "I, uh, I was just thinking. Admiring the pumpkin. Looks different in the moonlight."

"I know," Mariko said. "I came out to see the moon too. Did you ever notice the way it washes all the colors into silver?"

"Umm."

"The harvest moon!
    Among us, none
        Has a face of beauty."

"What's that?"

"A poem."

"Doesn't sound like any poem I ever heard. Poems have to rhyme."

"No they don't."

JoBob had heard that the full moon makes people crazy. Maybe that's what had happened to Mariko. They'd been neighbors for years and years—ever since the Kawabatas had come back from Jap camp when the war was over. They were in the same class at school and they rode the same bus to school every day, and she'd never said more than two words to him. He knew she could talk because she talked in class, when she was called on, but if it hadn't been for that he would have wondered. And now here she was, not just talking, but quoting poems *and* telling him that he didn't know what a poem was. But he did. They read poems in school, and they all rhymed.

"Yes they do," he said. "You read the same ones I did."

"Those were English poems," she said. "This one is Japanese."

This was getting too complicated for JoBob. He turned up the collar of his jacket, deciding that it was time for him to go. But he didn't really want to.

Mariko stood at the other end of the garden, silent too. Every other girl he knew couldn't *stand* quiet. They'd giggle or start babbling about something dumb at exactly the time when they should have been quiet.

JoBob let the silence come to its natural end. Then he said, "Doesn't make much sense."

"It does if you give it time," she said. "It's not like a story where everything's all spelled out for you. You have to think about it. Then the meaning will open up, sort of like a bud just naturally opens into a flower. You know?"

"Kind of. Could you say it again? So . . . so it might open up for me?"

"The harvest moon!" she began.

He liked the sound of her voice. When she was finished they were quiet again. JoBob thought about the poem—"Among us, none has a face of beauty"— and decided it was not true. The moon does, he thought, and Blue. He considered telling her about Blue, and the way he'd been feeling about the pumpkin just before he'd realized she was there. He'd learned a long time ago not to let on about those kinds of feelings. His mother said he was weird and his father said he was worse than a girl. But he had an idea that Mariko might know what he was talking about. Dummy, he told himself; she'll just laugh.

The door of the Kawabatas' house opened, sending a shaft of light into the garden. Mariko turned from a silvery wraith into a regular old girl, dressed in a navy blue jacket and blue skirt, her black hair glossy in the house light.

"Mariko? You all right? Who was it?"

"Just JoBob," Mariko said to the figure in the doorway.

So, he thought, she wasn't admiring the moon at all. They sent her out to see about the truck. He wanted to kick the pumpkin into a lot of squishy pieces. What a liar she was! He should have known better. They were just "dirty Japs," like his father said, couldn't trust them any farther than you could throw them.

"Good night, JoBob," Mariko called.

JoBob didn't answer. He turned up the collar of his jacket and walked fast down the road. He turned into his yard, threading his way through the junk. Out back some of his father's cocks crowed. A light-colored shape blurred in the darkness—Flea, his shepherd-mix bitch. "Hush, girl," he said, "it's just me." She whimpered in recognition, her entire hind end wagging along with her tail. She rolled over and JoBob squatted to scratch her stomach. He didn't want to go inside yet. He was still savoring what had happened at the barn, and when he went inside there'd be the racket of the TV if his parents weren't yelling at each other, or his sister, Darlene, talking on the telephone. The wind whistled across the fields, cold as winter, and maybe it was the wind that blew a Dark One into his mind.

The Dark Ones were another thing he never talked about to anyone in his family. They happened all by themselves, like dreams, and when he was little they scared JoBob to death. Then one day he said, "I know you. You're just a Dark One. Go away now." That particular one did go away. They still came—not as often as before—and they weren't so scary either, as if they were satisfied to be named and recognized. Sometimes they were things JoBob already knew way back in some corner of his mind, though he often didn't *want* to. Other times—like this one—they weren't specific. Just vague and ominous and made him feel creepy all over. JoBob shivered and told it to go away. All of a sudden he wanted to be inside where it was light and warm. Dark Ones hardly ever came into the house.

30

"That you, JoBob?" his mother called as soon as he let himself in.

"Yeah."

"Where you been?"

JoBob went to the door between the kitchen and the front room. "At the barn." The light from the TV flickered across Darlene, sitting on the couch doing her nails, his mother sitting on the other end of the couch with some mending in her lap, his father in the easy chair with his bad leg up on a stool. He had the latest issue of *Grit and Steel*, his favorite cock-fighting magazine, sitting on his lap. It wasn't open and he wasn't reading it. He didn't look up when JoBob came to the door, which meant that he was in one of his black moods. When he was in one of those he'd sit for hours in that chair, not talking or responding to anything that went on around him. That was fine with JoBob. At least he wasn't in a rage, so he wouldn't light into JoBob.

"In the middle of the night?" his mother asked.

"It's not even eight o'clock yet," JoBob said. "I don't call that the middle of the night."

Darlene got up and turned the volume up on the TV.

"Turn it down," his mother said.

"Can't hear with you yakking," Darlene said.

His mother got up and came through the door into the kitchen. "You must be starving," she said to JoBob while she examined the pots on the stove.

"I am," JoBob said. "What's for supper?"

"Just some of this old meatloaf. You don't mind it cold, do you?" She went on without waiting for him to answer, "And grits. I'll fry them up. They taste like glue when they're cold."

JoBob sat down at the table and watched her as she sliced a slab of grits and lit the flame on the stove. "Guess what happened today?" he asked.

She turned and looked at him. "Something good? You look like the cat got loose in the dairy."

"Better than that," he said. "I got a horse!"

"Well that's nice, honey. That's real nice." She smiled, but even though she was smiling and even though JoBob was excited about Blue, he noticed how tired she looked. Then her smile turned to a frown. "But how are you going to pay for a horse? Horses are for folks can afford them—rich folks like Trumaine Watson's."

JoBob explained that Slim had given Blue to him because he'd done such a good job training him, and how he was going to work to pay for the board.

"Well, I don't know," she said. "Don't do to go gettin' a swell-head, to start up thinkin' you're somebody you're not. Gettin' notions." This was one of her favorite expressions and she trotted it out on all sorts of occasions. He should have guessed this would be one of them.

"I won't."

"How come Slim decided to be so generous all of a sudden? I doubt if he did it for his health."

"I told you," he said. "Because I did such a good job training Blue and all."

She set JoBob's plate down on the table and sat down opposite him. "Well then *he* must have some notions." That would be some kind of underhanded notion, which was different from the kind she'd just been talking about that JoBob might have.

"Not everybody is like Pop," JoBob said.

"And what does that mean?"

"*He* wouldn't give anything away. Unless it was worthless. Or there was something in it for him."

She shot him a warning look, then pressed her lips together the way she did when she was arguing with his father. It's what she did when she knew she was right, but nobody was going to admit it. "That's enough."

JoBob should have known better. *She* could rant and rave about his father, but let him say one word and she'd . . .

Sure enough. "You better remember the Fifth Commandment. 'Honour thy father and thy mother; that thy days may be long in the land which the Lord thy God giveth thee.' "

JoBob poured syrup over his fried grits and said, "Yes, ma'am." He thought you ought to honor things—people—who deserved it, but he knew there was no use arguing with her over that one. When she started in on the Commandments it was time to shut up.

She stood up and smoothed her skirt. "Wash your dishes when you're done." Then she did one of those things that were always throwing him off-kilter. She put her hand on his head and stroked it gently. "It is nice."

"What?"

"About the horse."

JoBob swallowed hard. "Thanks, Mom."

She smiled then and went into the front room,

her house shoes going flap, flap across the kitchen floor. Soon JoBob could hear her and Darlene laughing along with the tinny laughter from the TV. He opened a can of peaches and ate them while he thought about calling Trumaine and telling him about Blue. He was still trying to decide whether to call him and tell him now, or leave it till morning, or leave it till afternoon when they got to the barn, as a sort of surprise, when the telephone rang—one long and two shorts—their ring.

JoBob scrambled up to answer it, thinking it was Trumaine, thinking that Trumaine had guessed—or knew somehow—that JoBob wanted to talk to him. It wouldn't be the first time such a thing had happened. He nearly collided with Darlene, who raced in from the front room. Nothing could get her moving like a ringing telephone.

"Hello-oo," she said in the new breathy voice she'd been practicing. It was sexy, she said, like Marilyn Monroe. JoBob thought she sounded silly. Her normal voice, even with the Oklahoma twang they'd gotten from their father, sounded a lot better.

JoBob stood beside her, waiting to see who it was. Maybe it *was* for him, even if nine times out of ten it was for her.

"Oh, *hi*," she said in the same fake voice and put her hand on her hip as if Parnell could see her. It was easy to figure it was Parnell, because she kept on in the same fake voice. Sighing, batting her eyelids, and shifting from one pose to another every few minutes. She still managed to glower at JoBob and look meaningfully at the stairs up to his room.

34

He made a face at her. Then he sat down at the table again and fished the last peach out of the can. He wasn't going to give her the satisfaction of having the room to herself. Besides, sometimes her conversations were pretty juicy. He couldn't believe she said things like that on the telephone when you could bet your bottom dollar that if Mabel Tompkins down the road wasn't listening in on the party line, Edna Nixon, the operator, was.

Parnell was the latest in Darlene's long string of boyfriends. He was pretty cool, JoBob had to admit—twenty-two, with his hair slicked back into a DA, the cigarette pack stuck into the rolled-up sleeve of his T-shirt, and his Levi's slung so low on his hips JoBob wondered why they didn't fall off. He played lead guitar in a group called the Cool Cats that played gigs all around the Sacramento Valley. Darlene said they were talking to an agent in Hollywood. Pretty soon they were going to get out of this dump and hit the big time. Be on the "Ed Sullivan Show," cut lots of records and they would all be Gold. And when all this happened—according to Darlene—she was going with them. And when she got there she was going to be Discovered. Sign a contract with Twentieth Century Fox and be on her way. JoBob wondered. If Parnell was such hot spit why would he mess around with *her?* Then again—Darlene was kind of hard to figure. She sure could make up some good stories. And she'd had some boyfriend or another almost as long as he could remember—each one in some way better than the last—which was more than he could understand. *He* sure wouldn't ask her for a date, much less ask her to go steady, but then she was his sister. She was pretty, he supposed, but he bet she'd lose her looks the way their mother had.

Sometimes he'd look at the wedding picture on top of his parents' bureau. On the bottom of the silver frame it said, Gavin McKenna Draper–Cerise Epson Draper. Underneath that, in scrolly lettering with a heart on either side, "Til Death Do Us Part. June 10, 1937." And the picture: his father, tall and handsome with his shock of black hair and broad shoulders, in a pale gray sharkskin suit with a foot cocked on the running board of the Model T and his arm flung around his mother's shoulders. She had her face tilted up, as if she'd been looking at him the moment before, and had turned her eyes to the camera at the very instant the photographer said "say cheese." Her hair curled around her face in soft wisps and she looked beautiful, but a little bit tentative too, as if a lot of questions were running through her head. As if, even then, she wasn't so sure whether Gavin's castles in the air were real or not. Nothing had happened to his mother that he could put into words. She was still slender and her hair was still soft and curly. Her complexion was peaches-and-cream, and she didn't have wrinkles like Trumaine's mother did; but she looked worn-out. Not pretty; as if now she knew about the castles. And they weren't real.

JoBob looked at Darlene and decided it wasn't fair. She'd gotten one good thing from their father—her height. She was nearly five feet eight inches tall, which was awfully tall for a girl. Yet she wasn't beefy, like their father, but willowy. JoBob had Gavin's black hair and blue eyes, which were so dark they were almost violet, but it sure didn't look like he was ever going to be six feet tall. Or even five feet eight inches. He'd been one of the smallest kids in his class as long as he could remember. "You'll grow," his mother said. But when? He was fourteen. His voice had changed—pretty much. He had a fairly respectable mustache when he didn't shave. But he was still five foot two.

All of a sudden JoBob was tired. Tired of listening to Darlene, and tired in his body too. It had been the most exciting day of his life, but Slim and his mother acted like it was something that happened every day—about as noteworthy as brushing your teeth. JoBob pitched the peach can into the trash, made a last face at Darlene, and went up to his room. He couldn't wait for morning. He couldn't wait to tell Trumaine and K.T. that he had a horse now. They'd have some proper enthusiasm. And he couldn't wait to tell Blue too.

4
■■■

THE KNOWLEDGE—and the words—seemed to build up in JoBob all night long, and when the school bus stopped for Trumaine in the morning JoBob knew he'd never be able to wait until they got to the barn in the afternoon to tell him. As soon as Trumaine sat down beside him, the words came spilling out. Trumaine grinned and punched him on the arm. Then JoBob told him that it was Blue and Trumaine looked puzzled. "He's just a lesson horse," he said. "What do you want him for?"

"He's a good jumper," JoBob said. "Even Slim said so." He told Trumaine the whole story and by the time he was through Trumaine was back to looking pleased.

Then he said with a small frown, "How come you never let on? How come you never told me?"

JoBob and Trumaine were easy together, but they'd been friends so long that they took a lot of things for granted, and let a lot of others slide under the rug. JoBob blushed. "I don't know. It started out sort of by accident. I brought him extra feed because he was so skinny. Then I tried riding him, just to see if maybe he could jump, and then it was already happening. *Had* already happened, sort of, so . . ."

"I wouldn't have told," Trumaine said. "I could have helped."

JoBob knew this was true, but he'd enjoyed doing it by himself. Without help from anyone. He made a soft fist and nudged Trumaine lightly on the upper arm. "So what do you think? You're not mad?"

"No," Trumaine said, "I think it's great. We're going to have some good times." Then he reared back in his seat and sang "Come on, baby, let the good times roll! Roll all night lo-ong!" He flung his head back and shimmied his shoulders. JoBob joined in and so did the kids across the aisle, and in the seats in front of them—all the kids their age and younger. Everyone sat on the bus according to age, youngest in the front, oldest in the back. "Come on baby! . . ."

"Shut it!" boomed a voice from the back of the bus. It was one of the senior boys sitting on the long seat in the back, which they reserved for themselves.

"Oh well," Trumaine shrugged. "They *will* be good times."

"They're going to be great times," JoBob agreed. "Remember how we watched K.T. jumping that big black gelding the first day we ever went to the barn? I didn't even know what a gelding was—but I knew he was black and I'd never seen anything so beautiful. How we swore we were going to do that one day, too?"

39

Trumaine nodded. "You swore, Joseph R. You were the one wanted to do it so bad you could pop. Me—" he shrugged. That was the way Trumaine was. Not too serious about anything, but he always went along with what JoBob wanted to do. Like calling him Joseph R. JoBob's name really *was* JoBob—that's what it said on his birth certificate—but JoBob thought it was a dumb cracker name, just the sort of thing his father would think up. So he decided that he would be called Joseph Robert, pretending that was his real name; but Trumaine was the only one who ever called him that. And half the time even Trumaine forgot.

"I never thought I'd have my own horse, though," JoBob said, feeling that it was too good to be true. Maybe he'd just dreamed it. All of a sudden he wanted to get to the barn. See Blue, have Slim confirm it; make sure that it really was true.

"He know yet?" Trumaine asked, pointing backward with his thumb. "He" was K.T., who was sitting with the rest of the senior boys. They were all pretty cool, and K.T. was the coolest, with his legs stuck casually out in the aisle and his father's RAF cap tilted down over his forehead. K.T.'s father had shot down three Messerschmitts in the Battle of Britain before one of them got him. JoBob wondered what it would be like to have a hero for a father, even if he was dead. He never let on that his father had been 4-F in the war, hadn't even tried to join up.

"Haven't had the chance," JoBob said. "Reckon he'll be tickled pink."

"Maybe he will," Trumaine said with a strange look, "and maybe he won't."

40

Trumaine liked to play the clown. He even looked a bit like one, with his bright red hair and baggy clothes, and often he acted like one, let on like he didn't really know what was going on, shrugging things off with a laugh and a joke. Underneath, though, his mind was working and he was observing. Old Trumaine didn't miss a lot, but it wasn't always easy to tell whether he was being serious or silly. So what did he mean? Why wouldn't K.T. be pleased?

Ever since they'd first started hanging around the barn, K.T. had helped them out. He was three years older and had been riding since he was a little kid. He knew a lot they didn't, so it was natural that he would help them out. Then, too, he said it was nice to have a couple of guys around instead of him being the only one in a sea of girls. In the four years since JoBob and Trumaine had been riding, the three of them had been through a lot together.

That afternoon, when the bus pulled up on Highway 99 by Gustavo's house, K.T. said, "Race you to the barn." He jumped off the bus and was running down the road while JoBob was still on the bottom step of the bus. Since he was a foot taller than JoBob and a good six inches taller than Trumaine, the winner was a foregone conclusion—even without a head start.

JoBob jogged down the road beside Trumaine. "Don't see why he has to do that," JoBob grumbled.

"He likes to win, that's all," Trumaine said.

"Everybody does," JoBob said, "but he has to win *all* the time."

"Oh well," Trumaine said with a shrug and a grin,

41

"today it seems like you're the winner."

JoBob grinned back and decided that Trumaine was right.

Slim and Irma Goldstein and Mel Hackett were sitting in their usual place, on the bench in front of the barn.

"Reckon you all heard the news," Slim said.

"What news?" K.T. asked. "What's wrong?"

"News ain't necessarily bad," Slim said, "and this here is good. Didn't you tell him, son?" he asked JoBob.

"Nope," JoBob said. "I thought it'd be a better surprise this way."

"Come on," K.T. said, "what is it?"

"JoBob's got a horse," Slim said. "Something that might even give Charlie a run for his money. Or Irma's mare."

"Well, that's real nice," Mel said.

"Where'd you find him?" K.T. wanted to know.

"Right here," Slim said.

K.T. looked puzzled. "There's not a horse on the place as good as Charlie. Not even Samantha." He turned to Irma, "Don't want to bad-mouth your horse, Irma, but you know it's true."

Irma nodded in agreement. "Well, how about Locomotive?" she suggested, naming the best of the lesson horses. He was good enough that Slim took him to shows sometimes. He knew the ropes, took care of the kids who were just starting out, and was a pretty good jumper.

"That new bay mare?" Mel put in. "The four-year-old come in last week from Fresno?"

42

They went on talking like that, with Mel and Irma and K.T. doing the speculating, while Slim and Trumaine and JoBob listened. JoBob was enjoying the tail end of his secret, knowing that within a minute or two it would be common knowledge.

Finally Irma said, "I swear we've named every horse on the place."

Mel turned his hands palms up. "You're pullin' our legs, Slim. It was a good joke, gettin' us to review all the stock you've got. Now, give. You found a little wonder in a pasture somewhere and you've been holdin' out, right?"

"Nope," Slim said. "We're talkin' about the last of them Colorado horses. The paint."

Mel and Irma looked surprised and K.T. burst out laughing. JoBob wanted to punch him out.

"Wait 'til you see him jump," Slim said with a warning look at JoBob, "then see whether it's still so all-fired funny."

All *right*, JoBob thought, unclenching his fists. When Blue jumped it didn't make one bit of difference what color he was.

"Okay," Slim said, "the day's not gettin' any longer. K.T., you get Charlie, and Trumaine, you get your mare. I'll set a few fences and you'll see what that little horse of JoBob's can do."

"You mean he's his?" K.T. asked.

"That's what I said," Slim said. "After the work he's done, I reckon he's earned it." Then he turned to JoBob. "Reckon he's earned a place in the barn, too. You want to get him out of that corral and put him in a stall?"

"I sure do."

"Okay," Slim stood up from the bench and walked inside the barn along with JoBob and K.T. and Trumaine. He lifted his hat and replaced it again, his thinking gesture. "I just got to think where to put him." He was wearing the gray Stetson for the first time that year. JoBob noticed that with a sinking feeling. The gray Stetson was Slim's winter hat, and JoBob didn't feel ready for winter yet.

K.T. and Trumaine went down the aisle to get their horses and Slim walked along with JoBob. "Here," he said, stopping at the stall next to Samantha. "I knew there was an empty stall along here somewheres. Now you go get Blue. And put a saddle on him. Reckon he can jump with a saddle on?"

"Don't see why not," JoBob said. "It's supposed to be easier, isn't it?"

"Supposed to be." Slim paused, then added, "Tempers and horses got no place together."

JoBob fidgeted with the halter he had in his hand. Slim sure didn't miss much. He knew how bad JoBob had wanted to light into K.T. He probably would have, too, if Slim hadn't been there.

"I know," JoBob said. "But horses aren't mean." When he was riding he *was* cool. He never got mad at the horses he rode. They depended on him and if you treated them right, they treated you right.

"Neither are people," Slim said. "For the most part. Besides, there's more than one way to skin a cat."

JoBob sighed. He wished Slim was right. "Like what?"

"Oh shoot. Talking. Thinking. Being smart."

44

"Yes, sir."

Slim gave him a little nod and JoBob went out to the corral to get Blue.

He led him out of the corral and into the barn, telling him how much he was going to like it in his new home. He tied him to the ring in his stall and started in on him with the currycomb. His own stall! He bet Blue had never had his own stall in his life. His coat would get sleek and shiny now that he didn't have to be outside all the time. JoBob gave Blue a good quick currying—he wished he could spend hours—but he didn't want to keep Slim waiting. Then he tacked him up, swung into the saddle, and headed out to the ring. It felt different with a saddle, and he felt a touch of sadness for all the times when he'd been alone with Blue, nestled into the warmth of his back, feeling all his muscles with his legs. "No matter," he told Blue. "I'll still ride you bareback sometimes. But today you've got to be really good again. Prove your worth. When Mel and K.T. and them see what you can do, they'll know you're blue chip all the way, right?" Blue arched his neck as he stepped out into the sun. JoBob reined him in tight and squeezed with his legs. Blue began to prance and JoBob glanced sideways to see if anyone was noticing. They were.

"Parade walk, eh?" Mel asked, and JoBob nodded, feeling proud. He'd taught Blue some other things that even Slim hadn't seen yet.

"He never looked like that in the lessons," Trumaine said.

"The rider maketh the horse," Slim said. "Now

45

stop ogling and get to work."

Trumaine worked Lulu along the rail for a few minutes and then started working her in circles to the left, curling concentrically into smaller and smaller circles, then out again, keeping her hindquarters on the same track as her forehand. Lulu was a pretty nice horse, but she was loose and too relaxed, didn't want to use her hind end, and this was aggravated by the fact that Trumaine wanted to be lazy too.

"I don't want to be," Trumaine had said more than once, "I just am." "Mind over matter," Slim said. "God gave you legs to *use*. Horse without his hindquarters engaged is like a car without a motor." Then he gave him the circle exercise and told him to work on it every day. "You wouldn't try driving a car without your foot on the accelerator, would you?" "Nope," Trumaine said. "Horse is no different," Slim said. "You need the gas, boy. Get that motor running. And you do that with your legs. You want to be a passenger, go down to the depot and get on a train."

JoBob wished that K.T. wasn't riding Charlie. Then he decided he'd better stop worrying about Charlie and start concentrating on Blue. K.T. wasn't worrying about *him*, he noticed. As far as he could tell, he hadn't even looked at Blue. JoBob played with the bit a little to get Blue's attention and started work in earnest. He wanted him to be warmed up and supple before they started to jump.

Slim made an X and they started trotting back and forth across it. It was the way they always started. JoBob knew it was important to do some warm-up jumps before they tackled the bigger fences, but Xs were boring. He must have trotted at least a thousand by now.

At last Slim said, "Okay, K.T., now canter around, jump that green and white vertical and then the coop."

K.T. collected Charlie around the turn, curled over the vertical, and cantered five smooth strides down to the coop. Nice.

Then Trumaine jumped the vertical and cantered down the line, nice and easy. Too easy. When she got to the coop Lulu came to a screeching stop. She planted her legs, lowered her head, and bugged her eyes out at the jump as if it were a rattlesnake.

"What's wrong?" Trumaine asked.

"You gotta get more impulsion than that," Slim said. "You need a hunter pace, not a snail's!"

Trumaine circled and jumped the vertical again, then headed for the coop, his face red with effort, his whole body working. But when they came to the coop, she stopped again.

"Hit her!" Slim yelled.

Trumaine hit her with his crop and she squealed and bucked.

"Circle," Slim said, "and hit her again, harder. Make her carry you through that line, and don't go bumping and grinding with your body like a Burly-que queen."

They all laughed. Trumaine gave her a good smack and this time she jumped through it, almost as nice as Charlie.

"See," Slim said. "She can do it just fine, but you've got to make her."

Now it was JoBob's turn. As he cantered along

the rail he realized with surprise that he was nervous, more nervous than he'd been last night when he was jumping for Slim. But he had a trick. He gathered up all the tension in his body and put it in a little sack in the corner of his brain. Then he drew the drawstrings tight around it, tied it with a square knot and let it lay. He looked ahead to the fence as he came out of the turn, and then they were over the vertical and cantering on down to the coop. They jumped the coop, nice and smooth, cantered off, and finished up with a circle at the end of the ring.

He pulled up and looked around. Mel put his hand to his forehead, then pulled it straight out and up in a salute. "You done somethin' there, JoBob," he said.

Trumaine said, "Boy, can he *jump!*"

"Real nice, JoBob," Irma smiled. "Real nice."

"See?" Slim said. "What did I tell you?"

JoBob grinned. It sure was nice to hear everyone saying good things about Blue. Everyone except K.T., that is. He was cantering Charlie in a circle, pretending to be preoccupied.

When the lesson was over, they walked out of the ring and down the road toward the pasture to cool out the horses before they put them away. In the woods along the pasture edge the elms and maples were sprinkles of scarlet and patches of yellow, the oaks a dusky umber, all the colors soft in the afternoon light. A wedge of ducks flew over their heads, so low they could hear the whir of their wings beating the air. The grass in the pasture rippled in the wind, washed gold by the long-slanting rays of the sun.

Trumaine kept looking at JoBob and grinning. "You weren't lying. He can jump, all right."

JoBob grinned back and stroked Blue's neck. "He likes to jump. He thinks it's fun. He's got a great disposition, too." It was more than fun, JoBob thought, his heart as light and free as the wild ducks, mere dots on the horizon now.

K.T. rode up so close to JoBob that their stirrups clanged together. "Too bad he won't get anywhere in the show ring," he said. "Too funny looking."

"He will too!" JoBob bristled. "Horses are judged on the way they jump, not their color. And there's nothing wrong with the way he jumps. You saw it with your own eyes."

"Well, I've got two more horses to ride." K.T. reined in Charlie and turned back toward the barn. "You all coming?"

"In a minute," Trumaine said. "Lulu's still a little hot." When K.T. was out of earshot he turned to JoBob. "See? What did I tell you?"

"But why?" JoBob asked. "Blue's not nearly as pretty as Charlie."

"Beats me," Trumaine said. "*I* think it's great you've got a horse now too."

"Thanks." JoBob beamed. Then they turned around too.

"He'll come around," Trumaine said.

They walked along the road back to the barn, their horses' hooves making a soft thunk, thunk in the dirt of the road. JoBob watched Charlie's round rump ahead of them, his tail swinging from hock to hock, and K.T., relaxed and easy in the saddle, his father's

RAF cap tilted at the usual angle.

"Just wait 'til we go to a show," JoBob said, half to Trumaine and half to K.T.'s retreating back. "We'll see what the judges think. They're the ones who count, right?" When he said the "right" he knew he wasn't talking to Trumaine or to K.T. either. He was talking to Blue. And himself.

5

■ ■ ■

ALL WINTER LONG JoBob bided his time. In the ring the ground was muddy, and the skies clamped down over the earth, gray and close as the lid of a kettle. The days were so short JoBob rode while it was still light enough to see, then he mucked his stalls afterward, with the rain drumming on the roof of the barn and the light outside a sheet of darkness. K.T. mostly ignored him, which was all right with JoBob. When spring came and the show season started up again, then he'd see what K.T. would have to say.

With Slim helping him now, Blue was getting better all the time. Better than even JoBob had thought he could get. JoBob was working two green horses for Slim too—a bay mare named Sophie Tucker and a chestnut named Twinkle—and Slim was pleased with the way they were coming along. JoBob was pleased too, but he wasn't attached to either of them the way he was to Blue. They were sale horses, anyway.

No sense in getting attached.

It was a long winter, but finally the storms slackened, the breezes in the valley smelled of the south, and the sun dried up the mud in the ring. Budding leaves swelled the branches of the trees, and wild mustard spread across the pale green of the hills, a jaunty, startling yellow. Prize lists for the spring shows appeared on Slim's desk with the entry blanks folded inside. JoBob and Trumaine took time on a Saturday afternoon in March to fill out the ones for the Silverado Riders Tenth Annual Horse Show, in Napa, the first one they'd decided to go to.

JoBob had already taken Blue to a schooling show, where he'd proved his worth. He got first or second in every class JoBob rode him in, which made them High Point for the show. JoBob was tickled. Slim said that proved he didn't need to screw around with any more tiddly-ass backyard stuff. He was ready for a big one. JoBob was excited, but when he added up the money for the entry fees he got worried. Fifty-five dollars! Almost as much as he'd saved up from working at shows all of last year.

"You can ride one show and work the next," Trumaine pointed out.

"I guess." JoBob thought it was unfair. He wanted to ride *every* show. Trumaine did, and so did K.T.

"The Lord helps those who help themselves," Jo-Bob's mother liked to say. Maybe Blue would win enough money so he could ride every show. Maybe he could work *and* ride—that would be helping himself, right? Or maybe the Lord would help him in some as yet unforeseen way. He stuffed the entry blank into the envelope and decided he might just be getting way ahead of himself. Maybe they'd bomb out. Or maybe K.T. was right. Maybe the judges would think Blue was too funny looking to pin him up where he deserved to be.

On the day before they were going to leave, JoBob got off the school bus and ran down the road to the barn with Trumaine beside him. K.T. sauntered along behind them. Seemed like he was always trying to be different. This day the excitement had been building up in JoBob all day—all winter, really—and doing something as sedate as walking, when Blue was waiting for him, was a flat impossibility.

He and Trumaine dropped their book satchels on the bench in front of the barn and stuck their heads into the office where Irma and Slim had their heads bent over the account books.

"Oatmeal cookies today," Irma said with a smile. She didn't need to point to the platter of cookies on the edge of the desk. JoBob had his eyes on them as soon as he looked into the office. Irma's husband had been killed at Omaha Beach at the end of the war and she didn't have any children. She called him and K.T. and Trumaine "her boys," and almost every day had a platter of cookies for them.

"My favorite!" Trumaine said.

"Thanks, Irma," JoBob said.

"You get on Twinkle first," Slim told JoBob. "She needs a little fine-tuning for the show. Then you can hack Sophie and wind up with Blue."

"Save the best for last?" Irma asked.

"Somethin' like that," Slim said.

"Yes, sir." JoBob said. He took three cookies and headed out into the barn.

"Hey, Blue," he called as he walked down the aisle. "Blue-oo!"

When Blue heard his voice he stuck his head over the stall door and whickered at JoBob. Every afternoon when he saw Blue's white face JoBob felt lighter, happier. He went inside and sat on the manger, gave one cookie to Blue, and ate the other two. No matter what the plan was for the afternoon, he always checked in with Blue first. Seemed like the right way to get school out of his system and horses into it.

When JoBob finished his cookies, he jumped down. "I've got to ride Twinkle now," he told Blue. "I'll be back for you later. Don't worry. We're going to a show tomorrow, remember?"

Blue flicked his ears, which told JoBob that he understood, and he went off to get Twinkle. When he was finished with her and Sophie, he came back for Blue. As soon as he led him out of the stall, he knew something was wrong. Blue was walking in a halting way, not at all like his usual swinging stride.

"Slim! Come quick!"

"What's wrong?" Slim yelled from the ring.

"Blue's lame." Just saying the words almost made him sick.

"Bring him out here and I'll take a look," Slim called back.

JoBob led Blue out of the barn and Slim came over from the middle of the ring.

"He's walking funny," JoBob said. "Something's wrong. *Really* wrong." Oh God, what if it was navicular, or founder, or . . . All of the permanent, incurable things that could happen to a horse jumped into JoBob's head at once and he'd never felt so awful in his life.

"Don't panic." Slim was calm. "Trot him down the road here and we'll see."

JoBob led him off at a trot, then turned and trotted back.

"You're right," Slim said, "he's a little off."

"A little off? He's dead lame!" Blue, Blue, please be all right, he told Blue silently. Blue flicked his ears back and forth to the sounds of JoBob's voice and Slim's, and stood with his left forefoot cocked.

"It's his left fore," Slim said. "That's clear." He picked up his foot and looked at it. Then he set it down, felt the ankle and tendons. "No heat or swelling," he said, "and that's a good sign. Reckon it's his foot. Might as well get Mel, though. See what he thinks."

JoBob handed the lead shank to Slim and went around to the back of the barn where Mel had his truck parked, with the forge glowing red hot and the anvil set up beside it.

With Mel watching, JoBob took Blue and trotted him back and forth again. Mel and Slim discussed it, then Mel went to get his hoof testers. When he tried them on Blue's left front foot, Blue rared back, his eyes rimmed white with pain.

"Okay, Blue," Mel said in a soothing voice. "I won't do it again."

"What's wrong?" JoBob asked.

Slim and Mel conferred for a few minutes, then Mel went back to the horse he'd been shoeing and

Slim said, "It's his foot, all right. Either a stone bruise or a gravel. Either way, it's a long way from his heart and he'll get over it. Should be fine in a week or two."

"A week or two?! But what about the show?" JoBob wanted to cry, or yell, or something. He'd been working for months and months and now *this*.

"Calm down," Slim said. "It ain't the only show in the world. There'll be others."

"But I've already paid the entry fees and I've been looking forward to it for weeks. For *months*."

Slim raised his eyebrows. "If I was you I'd be thinking about my horse, instead of one little disappointment."

"Little! It's not little. Don't you understand?"

"I understand, all right. Thought you were a better horseman than that." Slim's voice was hard.

"I . . ." JoBob stopped and swallowed hard. Slim was right. He'd been on the verge of getting mad at Blue. It wasn't his fault. "I'm sorry," he said to Slim and to Blue. "Guess I should be glad it's not something serious."

"You sure as hell should. Tell you what, you can take Sophie to the show instead of Blue."

"There isn't any 'instead of'!" He felt like yelling again.

"Simmer down," Slim said mildly. "You don't want to take Sophie, we can get a vet certificate and you can get your money back. But if I was you, I'd take Sophie. It'll be good experience for you."

"I guess." JoBob took Blue back to the barn feeling that he'd betrayed Slim and Blue, getting so disappointed about the show that he'd lost his perspective.

"I'm sorry," he told Blue again. "Shows go on all year long. It's just . . . Oh, phooey. Just nothing. I'm sorry, I really am." Blue dropped his head and looked mournful. JoBob thought how nice it was that it wasn't something serious. He wished he could do something to help Blue get better, but there was nothing he could do. If it was a stone bruise it would get better by itself in a week or two, just like a bruise on a person; and if it was gravel, the gravel would work its way up through Blue's hoof, then pop out the coronary band and he'd be fine. JoBob knew that. He'd seen lots of horses in the barn with both conditions.

He couldn't do anything for Blue's foot, so he made him a warm bran mash, which would be good for his spirit. Blue loved a bran mash, and if he was going to be laid up for awhile it would help prevent him from getting colic. JoBob's mind started going again, thinking about what would happen if he got colic, started rolling when no one was there, ended up with a twisted gut, and . . . No, he told himself firmly, it was no big deal. Blue was going to be fine. "You're the only horse I've got," he told Blue while he hung the bucket with the mash in it in his stall. "So you get better, and I'll see you when I get back."

Blue nuzzled JoBob's hand, then put his nose into the bucket, making peaceful chewing sounds.

JoBob had a good time at the show and he won some good ribbons with Sophie and Twinkle. Slim said he was turning into a mighty fine rider. "Not many people, short of a pro, could take two mares different as these and make it work." Twinkle was willing, but not very talented; whereas Sophie had a lot of ability, but was so timid she didn't know what she could do. So JoBob had to give her the confidence she didn't have for herself. JoBob didn't think it out ahead of time in words. He just did with his body what seemed to be required at the time. When Slim said things like that, it made him proud, like maybe he'd done more than he knew he had. He felt that all was right with the world—if Blue was all right, that is. Riding horses like Sophie and Twinkle made him realize what a good horse Blue was. Not very many had the ability *and* the desire.

When they got home from the show on Sunday night, there was a note from Mel on the blackboard: "Blue popped a gravel this aft. Sounder than a dollar." All *right,* JoBob thought, and went home feeling that things were indeed all right with the world.

The next day he and Trumaine decided to celebrate by taking Lulu and Blue on a trail ride down to the river. JoBob decided to go bareback, for old times' sake, and it was wonderful to be riding Blue again. They walked through the pasture with Blue striding along, strong and sound. He tossed his head and pranced, delighted to be out of his stall. When they got to the river they took off the bridles and let the horses graze while JoBob and Trumaine lolled in the grass. The willow trees drooped their feathery branches over the river, and the sound of the water was as peaceful as a lullaby. Going to a show with Blue would be great, but it was hard to imagine anything better than he had right then—a warm spring day, a good friend, and the best horse in the world.

March turned to April and, as the days grew longer, JoBob took extra time with Blue. In the schooling sessions, when JoBob jumped him, he was fresh and eager and was jumping better than he ever had. JoBob decided that maybe that gravel was a blessing in disguise. The rest had been good for him. A couple of weeks after the Napa show, they filled out the entry blanks for the Sacramento Horsemen's Association Spring Show, which would take place the last week in April. It would be Blue's first big show and he was ready. Was he ever!

6
■■■

WHENEVER JoBob thought about that show, a little curl of excitement would begin to unwind in his stomach. On Tuesday, the day before they were going to leave, JoBob gave Blue an extra good grooming and made him a bran mash. Blue was sound and this time they really were going. JoBob hung the bucket of mash on the hook in Blue's stall and said, "Okay, Blue, this is it. Tomorrow we're going to the show. That will be schooling day, which doesn't really matter—except a lot of people will be watching. After that, though—Thursday and Friday and Saturday and Sunday—it will matter. Besides all the other people, the *judge* will be watching. And deciding. About you."

He moved closer and curled his fingers into Blue's mane. Blue took his nose out of the bucket and rubbed his face on JoBob's chest. He knew how important it was. JoBob stroked both sides of Blue's neck with his hands. "Okay, buddy. I'm counting on you." Outside his stall JoBob turned around and said, "And

60

you can count on me. We'll do the best we know how." Blue flopped his ears back then, as if he knew he could relax, and turned back to the bucket of feed.

JoBob walked home so excited he couldn't keep quiet. He sang, "Off we go, into the wild blue yonder, flying high, into the sky! Off we go . . ." He tramped along the path through the woods, singing and singing, not caring that his voice shifted randomly between alto and tenor. There wasn't anyone to hear him. He wondered where it was going to end up. Baritone, he hoped, like his father's. He had his father's black hair and blue eyes. Maybe he'd have his voice too. When his father was in a good mood he'd get out his accordion and sing the Irish ballads his grandfather had taught him. The words were mostly sad—all about shipwrecks and treachery, lost loves and broken hearts. But JoBob didn't pay much mind to the words. He opened his ears to the tunes, which were sweet and melodious and lilted through the whole house. When his father was in a good mood like that JoBob almost forgot what he was like the other times.

He stopped for a moment and tried some do-re-mis, going down as far as he could. He'd turned fifteen more than a month ago and he had decided that after his birthday his voice would stop cracking. "Do, ti, la, so—" Just when his voice was getting deep and rich with some real resonance to it, it cut out on him. He shrugged and went on. This evening he felt too good to let it bother him. And it *was* happening less often.

For now he moved up an octave and sang as he walked along:

I ride an old paint, I lead an old Dan
I'm goin' to Montana to throw a hoolihan
They feed in the coolies, they water in the draw . . .

That song made him smile inside. He rode a paint,
all right, but he wasn't old and he was goin' to the
Sacramento Fairgrounds to show the horse show world
just what he could do. All of a sudden, maybe because
it was such a mournful tune, his throat caught and
he felt like crying. He thought of the cowboy singing
that song to his cattle with the wide prairie sky stretching above him like the wings of a great dark eagle,
the cattle lowing, restless, and the cowboy all alone
out there, singing not just to his cattle, but to himself
too, to keep the loneliness at bay, to keep himself
from thinking of a warm house with someone to talk
to. . . .

Almost as if his thoughts had made it happen, he
heard a clear sweet soprano voice singing:

Ride around, little dogies
Ride around 'em slow . . .

Sometimes when he was daydreaming he could see
the things going on in his head as vividly as a movie,
but this was the first time he'd ever *heard* anything.
He shivered, and it wasn't the evening cool that made
him shiver. If you heard things that weren't there,
that meant you were crazy.

But the voice went on and finished the chorus,
and by then JoBob was convinced that it was real.
The voice even sounded familiar, though he couldn't
quite place it.

62

Who was it? He started to move toward the sound, then he had a better idea. He stood where he was and sang the next verse. When he was through he waited for the other to sing the last one. Just when he was wondering if maybe he hadn't imagined it after all, the notes of the last verse came through the trees off to his right, not too far away. In fact, he thought he glimpsed a patch of navy blue. When the last notes died away he threaded his way through the trees, and emerged into a little clearing. She'd been close, all right, not more than ten yards from the path. She stood in the clearing facing him—Mariko in a navy pea jacket and Levi's with the evening light filtering through the trees and dappling her hair. She had a basket on her arm and when she saw JoBob she smiled.

"That was fun," he said.

She nodded. "Sounds better without Mr. Willoughby yelling, 'And one! Altos, I can't *hear* you!'"

"Yes. It's kind of an outdoors song, anyway." It was true. It sounded a lot better out here in the woods than it did when they were singing it in music class.

She looked at JoBob. She wasn't smiling, or frowning either. Just looking at him. Well, two could play that game, so he looked back at her. All of a sudden, for no reason he could figure out, he found himself blushing.

"What are you doing here?" he asked, hoping to distract her so she wouldn't notice him blushing.

"Picking mushrooms for supper," she said, raising the basket in her hand.

"Are you kidding?" He stepped closer and looked

into her basket. "Those are toadstools. You eat those? They'll kill you."

"No, they won't. And there's no such a thing as a toadstool. They're all mushrooms. Some are poisonous, and some aren't. You just have to know the difference."

JoBob had been told so many times that all toadstools were poisonous that he didn't believe her. "How can you tell?"

"You only eat the ones you're positive about. Like these. They're called shaggy manes. See how they're sort of ruffly?"

JoBob peered at the cream-colored ovals nestled in her basket and nodded.

"They're delicious," she went on. "And unmistakable. No poisonous mushroom looks anything like a shaggy mane. And shaggy manes tend to grow in the same place, which makes it really easy. This clearing is my shaggy mane place. I've got them all now, though." She hooked her arm through the basket and started toward the path.

JoBob fell in beside her. He'd seen lots of toadstools, especially that year, but he didn't pay them any more attention than the rotting leaves and fallen tree branches. It had never occurred to him that they had names, or that anybody in their right mind would eat one. "How 'bout that one?" he asked, pointing to a large white one with a smooth rounded cap nestled among the gnarly roots of a big oak tree.

Mariko knelt and pushed the leaves away from the stem.

JoBob crouched beside her. "Well?"

She pulled the mushroom up, then turned it over

64

to look at the gills on the underside. "I don't know what this one is. Wouldn't dream of eating *it.*"

All of a sudden, JoBob noticed how shiny her hair was, even in the shadowiness of the woods, and how she smelled sort of fresh and outdoorsy without any of that garbagey perfume like Darlene used. He also noticed filaments of a spider web stuck in her hair and, without thinking, he reached out and brushed it off. Her hair felt as silky as it looked.

She dropped the mushroom and brushed her hands off, then reached for her hair. "What's wrong?"

"Just a spider web."

"That's what happens when you go poking around in the woods." She didn't giggle or flutter. She was looking right at him again, her eyes direct and dark, with a hint of laughter in them too.

Most girls wouldn't look at you at all, just brushed their eyes past you like you were some kind of bug. He sort of liked her looking at him like that, but it embarrassed him too. He didn't know why. She was just Mariko. No big deal. And yet . . .

He stood up. "It's getting late. I gotta go."

"Me too." She stood up too, then bent down to pick up the basket, and he noticed her bottom and her legs. Curvy, enticing. He'd never seen her in pants before or noticed what a nice figure she had.

They walked in silence for awhile, their feet scuffling the leaves on the path. JoBob was looking straight ahead, but he could see the top of her head out of the corner of his eye, and he thought she was just the right size. He hated it when girls were taller than he was.

After they'd been walking for a few minutes she

asked, "Is that your horse you were riding the other day? The pretty brown one with the white spots?"

"Where'd you see him? You spying on me?"

"No! I was looking for mushrooms in the big pasture that goes down to the river, over by Oak Knoll Farm. I just happened to see you."

"Chestnut," he said. "You don't call horses brown."

"Excuse *me.*"

"There are lots of special words for horses' colors," he went on real fast. "There are so many shades of, uh, brown, that they have different names: chestnut, bay, buckskin, palomino, and things like liver chestnut—a liver chestnut can be as dark as a bay, 'cept their mane and tail is the same color as the rest of their coat, whereas a bay always has a black mane and tail. . . ." He trailed off because she didn't seem too interested. In fact, she looked hurt. "Hey, I didn't hurt your feelings, did I?"

"Yes."

He was startled. He expected her to giggle and say no. But there it was. Just "yes." He wished she'd stop being so disconcerting, act more like a normal girl. No, he decided, it was exactly because she was so . . . so herself that he was . . . what was he? Well—"I'm sorry," he offered. "I didn't mean to."

"I guess not."

She didn't look mad, so JoBob went on. "Blue's sort of special and when I'm riding him in the pasture I feel alone. Sort of weird to think that I wasn't, that you were looking at me. . . ."

She nodded. "When you're outside by yourself you don't realize other people might be out there too."

"Right! It's one of the things I like best about riding

66

Blue down there by the river. It feels so good to be outside, free . . ."

Mariko nodded. "Wish I could feel that way all the time." She sounded wistful, and JoBob wanted to comfort her. Ever since that evening in October when she told him that poem about the moon, every now and then he'd notice her at school eating by herself in the cafeteria, or sometimes with a bunch of girls. But if she was with others, she'd be on the edge of the group—not chattering and laughing—but poised, like a deer in the woods, ready for instant flight. Sometimes, too, when they were waiting for the bus, he'd look at her, wanting to talk to her, but she didn't give him a chance. She was polite, the way she'd always been, but something about her manner told him to keep his distance. So he did. Then he'd *notice* her again, and he'd wonder what she was thinking.

"You could feel free," he said softly.

She gave him a strange look. "You don't know what you're talking about."

"Okay," he bristled. "Why don't you tell me?"

"You're a *gigenda*. You wouldn't understand."

"Well, I sure won't if you don't tell me."

"Because other people don't see you for yourself. They just see . . . They stare at you like you were some kind of sideshow freak, or they look right through you like you don't even exist. Say things about you while you're standing right there. But when I'm by myself, outside, there's no one else around and then, sometimes, I forget, I . . ." She stopped and bit her lip.

"Why don't you beat them up? That's what I did

to Butch Johnson and he stopped bugging me."

She gave him a withering look. "You don't understand."

"Stop saying that! I might if you tried to explain it. I can't read your mind, you know."

"Because you can't beat up the whole world. And you can't change peoples' minds, either. They'll think what they want to think, no matter what the truth is."

"Like Blue."

"What?"

"My horse. People are always making fun of him because he's a paint. They look at his color and don't think about what he can do. How he *is*."

There was a long silence. "That must be awful," he added.

There was another long silence and JoBob was afraid he'd said something wrong again. Finally she spoke in a low musing voice. "You really think so?"

"Yes."

"I'm surprised at you, JoBob. I thought . . ."

"What?"

She shrugged. "Oh, never mind. I'm talking too much."

"No, you're not." He wanted to say that she'd just started talking enough. To tell her how nice it was to be talking to her like that. How Darlene and the girls at school and at the barn were always jibbering and jabbering, but never said anything worth remembering. They never listened either. He wanted to tell her how it made him feel almost comfortable to be with her, like she might be a real friend. But he couldn't make himself say any of those things.

They emerged from the shadow of the woods into the fields stretching all the way up to the highway. It was the time of evening when the light gathered equally into the land and the sky, so the whole land-scape seemed to glow. He'd seen that land every day since he was born. Plenty of times he didn't notice it, any more than he noticed his school pencil or his shoes. They were all part of his surroundings, so familiar they'd dropped into a level where they were simply there. This evening, though, he *noticed*. Rosy wisps of cloud trailed across the sky, and the fields stretched before him, the dark loam of the soil traced with row upon row of strawberry plants like green ruffles sewn into the earth.

"Well," she said with a little smile. "Here's where we come to a parting of the ways."

"Yes." He was smiling too. She started down the path to her house and he stood watching as she swung along the path with a lithe, easy stride.

All of a sudden JoBob didn't want it to end. "Hey, Mariko," he called.

She stopped and he ran to catch up.

"Listen, maybe I could go looking for mushrooms with you sometime."

"All right," she said. "If you really want to. But you better not eat any. Toadstools are poisonous, you know." Then she grinned, waved her basket, and set off down the path again.

"A man who's got land is a rich man," his father liked to say. And this evening JoBob felt the rightness of it. He felt rich, not exactly money-rich, like Tru- maine must, but soul-rich. It was their land he was looking at.

Mariko was halfway up the rise to her house when JoBob spotted another person traveling along a path that intersected with hers. It was Tom Kawabata, her father, coming in from the fields with his hoe over his shoulder. When Tom and Mariko met, they stopped and faced each other. JoBob wondered what they were saying. Then they turned and walked on toward their house. The lights in their house, and his, were already on, sending a warm glow out into the dusk. JoBob wondered if Tom minded working land that belonged to somebody else.

"Hell no," his father had said when he asked him once. "Japs aren't used to owning things. Even in Japan they were just coolies, working for the Emperor or some fancy muckety-muck. Tom's not a citizen anyway. Can't own any good all-American land."

At the time JoBob had just said, "Oh," and hadn't thought about it much. Now he watched the two retreating figures silhouetted against the sky, their heads high, backs straight; and he thought that it didn't seem right, somehow. Why should Tom bust a gut, bending over those strawberry plants, while his father didn't do anything except potter around with his cocks and pocket a share of the money Tom made from the strawberry crop?

He was hungry and it was getting late and he had a million things to do to get ready for the show, but he wasn't ready to go into the house yet. He wanted to ask Mariko what a *gigenda* was. And he wanted

70

to tell her about the show. How excited he was, but worried too. He didn't let on to anyone at the barn that he was worried, but he was. And sometimes it helped to talk about it—if the person you were talking to didn't jeer. And he had a feeling that she wouldn't.

7
∎∎∎

J<small>O</small>B<small>OB</small>'<small>S</small> <small>EYES</small> traveled back across the fields, following the rows of strawberries to where they ended at the copse that enclosed the chicken runs behind the house. And the pit. JoBob was standing in one of the few places where you could see the pit from a distance. If a person came up to the house, the only thing they'd see was the house and all the junk in the front yard. Even if you walked out back, you wouldn't see anything except the woods. His father had taken care of the road to the pit, too. It came in from the highway up above the regular road to the house and looked like a tractor track meandering through the fields. On fight days, just in case, they posted a guard out on the highway by the upper road—not anyone that a body would notice—just an old guy in a rattletrap truck, but he had a walkie-talkie and if he saw anything threatening he called in to the guys down at the pit.

His father and Chet Masterson were standing near

the edge of the pit, Chet's red shirt and his father's blue one looking out of place among the greens and browns of the land. His father and Chet were partners of some kind, JoBob didn't exactly know what. They owned cocks together and every now and then worked other kinds of deals too. JoBob's heart sank. He wouldn't be able to get to the house without going by them and, as soon as his father saw him, he'd think of something for him to do. Something he didn't want to do, that was as surefire a bet as that the sun would rise in the morning.

Sure enough. "Hey, JoBob," came his father's voice. "Come on down here and give us a hand."

JoBob went.

"Go get Emerald," his father said, "and then you can play like the referee."

"Yes, sir." JoBob's stomach was in knots and it wasn't because he was hungry. He knew what was going to happen next and even though he'd seen it plenty of times, it still made him sick.

He went down the path between the chicken runs and came back in a few minutes with Emerald tucked under his arm.

"That's not Emerald, you idiot." His father's voice slashed through the air like a whip. "Take him back and get Emerald. And get it right, this time."

JoBob went back along the path, rage boiling inside him. He stopped outside Emerald's run and opened the door. At least he thought it was Emerald's run. It was where he'd always been before. He looked closely at the cock he was holding. He had the same bright green feathers on his neck and tail, sure looked like

Emerald. But now he noticed this cock was a bit smaller, he didn't have the battle scars Emerald did and his eyes were placid, without the lethal glitter that Emerald's had. JoBob put the cock back in the run and walked along looking for Emerald. He supposed his father had switched them on purpose, trying to trip him up—one of his little "jokes."

On the right-hand side, near the middle, he found Emerald. This time he looked real close, to make sure it really was Emerald. When he came back his father took Emerald from him and said to Chet, "You ever see such a dumb kid? Been around birds since he was born and still can't tell one from the other."

"Lay off," Chet said. "Just proves our point." His voice was mild, but JoBob noticed that he looked uneasy about something.

"I suppose it does," Gavin muttered. Then he set to work fitting the steel gaffs over Emerald's claws. He wasn't paying any attention to JoBob now, or Chet either; he was utterly intent on his work.

"Big fight up in Grass Valley on Sunday," Chet said, as if JoBob didn't know it.

JoBob tried not to look at the young speckled cock Chet held, and he tried not to notice that Chet wasn't putting any gaffs on him. Not that it would help much. He was one of the culls and he didn't know it, but in a few minutes he was going to be dead. Before a big fight his father took the culls and let the ones who were going to the fight have at them. "Gets their blood up," he said. "Whets their appetite."

JoBob took his position at the rim of the pit where

the referee normally stood. "Bill your birds," he sang out.

Chet with the speckled cock and Gavin with Emerald walked to the center line. There they stopped and held their birds out. Emerald hissed fiercely and twisted in Gavin's hands, trying to get at the speckled cock. He hissed too, but there was no bottom to it. No real fighting spirit. Which was why he was a cull. He'd never make it.

The two men backed off from the center line with the birds struggling in their hands. They crouched and let the birds touch the tamped dirt of the pit with their claws, while keeping them restrained with their cupped hands.

"Pit your birds!" JoBob hollered.

Almost before JoBob said "pit" Emerald was up, his wings whipping the air, his gaffs a glint of silver. Then he plummeted down onto the speckled cock. Emerald's gaffs sank into his back. With his wings still whipping furiously, he raked his claws across the back of the speckled cock. Trails of blood oozed on the speckled's back. Emerald beat off into the air again, then shot down again, this time going for the throat of the speckled one with his beak. Once, twice . . .

The speckled cock lay in the dirt, quivering, his head flopping at a strange angle, his eyes glassy, and the blood already pooling beneath him.

Emerald crowed triumphantly. Gavin grinned with satisfaction. "He'll do," he said, stroking the bright green feathers on Emerald's neck.

"Let's hope so," Chet said. "We've got a lot at stake this time."

"I know," Gavin replied. He started to say something else. Then he glanced at JoBob, and stopped. "Best cock I ever had," he went on in a too-loud voice. He tucked Emerald under his arm and walked along the path between the runs. "Nobody's going to take *him,* not even some fancy-dancy Peruvian bird. Peru. All they got down there is a bunch of spics can't even speak English. It'll be a shoo-in."

When they came to Emerald's run Gavin put him inside, then fastened the door carefully. The three of them walked along up the path toward the house.

"I just hope it works," Chet said. He sounded uneasy and JoBob noticed his pulse beating fast under the scar on his cheek.

After a minute Chet turned to JoBob. "You coming?" he asked. "It's going to be a real humdinger."

"I'd like to," JoBob lied, "but I'm going to be in Sacramento."

"Oh? You going to another horse show?"

"Yes, sir," JoBob answered, wishing that Chet would stop. Sometimes the mere mention of a horse show would send his father into a rage and JoBob had already had enough of that for one day.

"He's gotten too high-toned for us," Gavin said, real sarcastic. JoBob clenched his jaw and waited for him to light into him, but this evening he seemed to have something else on his mind. He looked at his watch and grabbed Chet by the arm. "Let's head on down to Riley's. Celebrate a little."

"Maybe we ought to wait until there's something *to* celebrate," Chet said.

"Shoot," Gavin said, draping his arm over Chet's

shoulder. "Like I said, it's going to be a shoo-in." Then he turned and looked back toward the chicken runs. "A shoo-in," he repeated in a hearty voice. Sounded like he was trying to convince someone, and JoBob wondered who it was.

8
■ ■ ■

WHEN JOBOB woke up it was still dark, but he knew in his bones that the night was nearly over. He switched on the light and looked at the clock. Five-thirty. Time to go. He dressed quickly, grabbed his suitcase, and was out the door in a jiffy. Flea greeted him with yelps of joy and capered around him in circles, her tail wagging fiercely. "Shh," he said, "hush, Flea," rubbing behind her ears to quiet her. Then he set off for the barn, the sky still dark, but pale and lightening along the horizon like the pearly inside of a seashell. The air filled with the chirps of awakening birds and the stirring of the trees. Flea trotted along beside him, flicking her ears, then dashed off on short forays after squirrels. Every step JoBob took away from his house made him feel better.

Last night he'd eaten supper and packed and gone to bed early, but some time in the middle of the night the racket downstairs woke him up. His parents arguing. He couldn't catch any words, just the tone:

78

his father's voice loud and bellowing; his mother's low and wheedling. He'd lain there, tense as a cat, clenching and unclenching his fists. He hated it when his mother sounded like that. When his father made her sound like that. He wished he could knock the shit out of his father the way he had Butch Johnson. Butch wasn't the biggest kid in their class, but he was by far the meanest, and just about everybody was scared of him—including JoBob. Butch liked to taunt people. He made fun of JoBob's accent and his size, called him "shrimp" and "hillbilly" and, worst of all, "Okie."

One day last year, though, Butch had made JoBob so angry that he wasn't scared anymore. He said, "Say that one more time and I'll punch you out." "Don't make me laugh," Butch said. "A shrimp like you? Just go on back where you belong, Okie." That did it. JoBob was on him. He was a lot smaller than Butch, but he was quick and strong, and he was so mad right then he could have tromped someone twice his size. He'd whomped Butch good that day. After that Butch didn't bug him anymore, and the other kids laid off calling him names too. But his father was meaner than Butch, besides being a whole lot bigger and stronger. So JoBob lay there with the anger spewing around in him, knowing there was nothing he could do.

By the time JoBob emerged from the woods into the pasture behind the barn, the sky along the horizon throbbed with the rosy promise of the sun. Overhead the last stars winked out into the sky, which was shading from gray into blue. JoBob set down his suitcase and sat on it, his hands around his knees. Flea dropped down beside him and nudged his forearm with her nose.

JoBob rubbed her ears, then pulled the note out of his back pocket. He'd found it on the kitchen table when he came down that morning:

> *Dear Son,*
> *Good luck at the show. Remember that Epsons always measure up, and* YOU'RE *an Epson.*
>
> *Love, Mom*

It was not strictly true, of course. *She* was an Epson; he was half an Epson. She always brought it up when she was expecting him to do something he almost certainly was not going to do, like make straight A's; or when he'd done something that made her proud. Then she'd start talking about how nice it was his Epson blood was finally showing—he hadn't gotten anything from the damn Drapers except his good looks and an idiotic Irish penchant for dreaming. Probably a weakness for drink too, just like the rest of them.

Like so many things his mother did, this note made him both puzzled and pleased. Ever since he'd had Blue, she'd listen to him talk with only half an ear, as if she wasn't quite sure that Blue existed. Or was it that she didn't care? So now . . . Why this interest, all of a sudden? Was she going to be proud if he did well? Or did she think it was an impossibility? Or was something else going on that he didn't have a clue about?

"*I* don't know," he told Flea. "I do know that I'll be glad to get out of here, even if it is just for five days." He fell silent and looked out over the fields. "Forever would be even better," he added.

Flea whimpered and nudged insistently at his arm. He stretched his hand down and scratched under her belly. "Don't worry. If I was leaving for good, I'd take you."

Then he looked out across the fields, trying to clear all this home stuff out of his mind. If his brain was all cluttered up with that, he wouldn't be able to ride worth spit. The alfalfa in the pasture spread in front of him, a carpet of pale green. Off to the west an old water tower shimmered in the morning light. And in front of him lay Oak Knoll Farm—the big red barn with the huge old live-oak tree towering over it and, by the main door, beside Slim's bench, the forsythia and bridal wreath, in bloom now, splashes of yellow and white. Sprawled around the big barn were the little barn, the machine shed, corrals, the ring.

"Just look at that, Flea," he said. "You ever see anything so nice?"

She answered with a small noise that sounded like a whimper. Except JoBob knew better. It was the noise she made when she wanted to bark and frolic, but thought she was supposed to keep quiet and be sedate.

In the lesson-horse corral the horses gathered at the gate waiting for Gustavo to come with their morning hay. They waited peacefully enough, but as soon as Gustavo showed up with the hay, they'd be pinning their ears and cocking their hind legs, running off the ones who wouldn't fight.

JoBob stood up. "It's a good thing Blue isn't there anymore," he told Flea. "Now you wish us luck."

Flea made the noise again and this time it *was* a whimper. She knew JoBob was leaving. He crouched beside her and tousled her ears. "Good girl," he said, "I'll see you on Sunday, hear?" Then he picked up his suitcase and said in a stern voice. "Go home. Go home," pointing at the path. She gave him a last reproachful look and went, her tail a white banner among the trees.

When JoBob walked into the barn Slim was already at work in the tack room, packing bridles and halters and show sheets into the big tack trunks. JoBob counted out buckets, stacked them, and carried them out to the van, where he added them to the pile of gear already waiting to be loaded.

By mid morning the van was packed, and the horses wrapped for the trip. JoBob brought the horses one by one for Slim to load into the van. Charlie and one of Slim's sale horses that K.T. rode went in first, their hooves clattering up the ramp, then came Lulu and Samantha, and, finally, Blue and Twinkle. They unhooked the side panels from the ramp and stowed them in the van. Then they slid the ramp into position under the bed and slid the doors shut. Slim walked around, double-checking everything, and then they were off!

After they'd turned onto the highway and the horses had settled, Slim glanced at JoBob. "You ready for this?"

"Sure. Who'd you say the judge was?"

Slim pushed his hat back with a fist on the forehead. "Yancy McClean. From Aiken, South Carolina."

JoBob stretched out his legs and jammed his hands into his pockets. "A back-East judge won't take to a pinto in the hunter division."

"What gave you that idea?"

JoBob shrugged. "I don't know. K.T., you . . ."

"I never bad-mouthed that horse since last fall. Not once. He's proved himself to me."

"Yeah, I know. I guess."

They rode in silence for awhile, then Slim spoke. "This old Yancy's got a fancy back-East address and a place down at Aiken with white fences and a barn with a brick floor and brass doodads on the stall doors, but—" He turned to JoBob and wagged his finger, and JoBob was dying to hear what Slim was going to say next, because his voice dropped down a couple of registers the way it did when he was going to say something important, but he was scared too, because Slim wasn't looking at the road at all and he was the sole person behind the wheel of that six-horse van, and Blue was in that van.

"—But," Slim went on, "Yancy and me know each other from way back when."

That could mean some time so far back it was probably medieval. It was also one of Slim's favorite expressions and whenever he said it, it made JoBob feel good, like there was bread dough rising on the stove top, its rich yeasty smell filling the whole house, a fire crackling in the fireplace, and a nice old crazy quilt draped over the rocking chair in front of the fireplace. Outside the winds might howl, and bears might be prowling around, but Slim would have his rifle standing on its stock right by the door; and inside it was cozy and warm and safe. . . .

"In the cavalry. At Fort Riley." That placed it in time, sort of. The cavalry had been disbanded in 1945 when JoBob was four years old. "And he wasn't fancier than spit," he finished.

Or had he finished? No. He'd been pushing his hat back a little bit at a time all along during the conversation and now it was out of its natural position, way far back on his head, so it exposed a couple inches of hair and a strip of white skin on his forehead that contrasted sharply with the deep tan on the rest of his face. Now he grabbed the brim and pulled it down onto his forehead, back into its usual place. And then he did finish: "You don't ride with someone for four years, eight hours a day, without finding out whether he knows a horse from a hole in the ground."

"And?" JoBob had to ask. It was the right time for him to say something, but he already knew what Slim was going to say—at least he thought he did.

"Yance knows a good horse when he sees one. And Blue is a good horse." Slim glanced at JoBob with a hint of a smile tweaking the corners of his mouth. "I planned it like this, you know. First time the show crowd sees Blue I wanted to be sure we'd have a judge who has an open mind."

They lapsed into silence and the van hummed along the highway. JoBob was gratified. He was more than gratified; he'd never felt so good in his life. "Thanks, Slim," he said, wishing he knew how to say it better.

Slim adjusted his hat. "Never mind," he said. "You

still gotta ride him."

Things were getting even better. Most of the time when things went bad on you, it was because something or another wasn't in your control. Another person threw a curve at you out of left field, or pulled the rug out from under you. But this time it was safe. All JoBob had to do was ride Blue, and he *knew* he could do that. Still, he dropped his right hand onto the seat where Slim couldn't see it and crossed his fingers, for luck. Slim thought that kind of thing was silly, but JoBob wasn't taking any chances.

"Now I want you to be real careful with Twinkle," Slim said. "She was real good at the Napa show, but with a greenie, you never know."

"I will," JoBob said. "I just wish she was a better jumper."

"I'll tell you somethin'," Slim said. "Horses are like people. Some got one kind of thing going for them, some got another. Twinkle's pretty as a picture and sweet as sugar. With a disposition like that, I'd trust her with my own grandmother. Ain't every horse can jump the moon, you know." There was a warning edge to his voice and JoBob wondered what he meant. Was he expecting too much? Not trying hard enough with Twinkle because she didn't have Blue's ability?

"You know the parable of the talents?" Slim asked.

"I heard it in church," JoBob said. "Stupid story. I don't think it's fair of the Lord to take away from the one servant what he had. Poor guy only had one talent to start with. So he buried it. He was doing the best he knew how, right? He was *trying.*"

"You missed the point," Slim said. "Point is you

85

gotta *use* what you got. And who ever told you life was *fair?*"

The van rolled into the fairgrounds and JoBob got to work. They had to unload the horses and all the tack and equipment from the van, bed down the stalls, put up the stall signs, and set up the tack room. JoBob was running around for hours, hammering in nails, setting up the saddle rack in the tack room, unwrapping the horses, filling their water buckets. . . . Then it was time to take a saddle out of the tack room where he'd stowed it not so long before, put it on a horse, and get up to the ring to school. It was exciting to be in the midst of so much activity, to see all the people he hadn't seen since the Napa show a month ago.

After they'd been there for an hour or two Irma drove up and started what Slim called fussing. She retied the curtains to the tack room, got JoBob to straighten the brass stall signs and polish them. JoBob didn't mind, although he'd polished them at home, a couple of days before they'd left.

It felt good to know that he was not in some hick barn. He liked having Irma there too. She always went up to the ring to cheer on "her boys" when one of them had a class, and did other nice things like sew on a button one of them might have popped off his jacket. When she was finished with the tack room they all stepped back to look. The new green curtains had "Oak Knoll Farm" across the top in fancy white lettering. On each horse's door was a stall sign, also in green and white, with the horse's name at the bottom and a stylized oak tree in the middle. And below each sign was a green and white show sheet. Irma went along refolding the sheets. Then she took some white chrysanthemums in green pots out of her car and arranged them in front of the tack room.

"What do you think?" she asked.

"It looks terrific," JoBob said.

"A body would think he was in *House and Garden* instead of a horse show," Slim grumbled, but he was pleased, JoBob could tell.

Just about everyone walking by stopped to compliment them, and then Slim beamed and allowed as how it did look pretty nice.

By midafternoon, when K.T. and Trumaine arrived, JoBob had already ridden Twinkle and Irma's mare, Samantha. Irma liked for him to ride Sammie on schooling day to get her tuned up. The way Irma rode, Sammie needed all the help she could get. JoBob had also lined up five stalls to muck, besides the ones he was doing for Slim. K.T.'s mother, and Trumaine's, said missing Thursday and Friday classwork on account of the show was bad enough, no sense in missing Wednesday too, just to school the horses. JoBob was glad that his mother didn't seem to care. He already felt settled in and on top of things when he spotted them wandering around, wondering where their barn was.

K.T. tacked up Charlie, Trumaine got on Lulu, JoBob got on Blue, and they headed up to the ring.

"Hey, JoBob!" Fonz Robertson called. "You still working?"

"You bet," JoBob said. "Got anything for me?" Fonz

was a Western trainer and JoBob had worked for him last year, cleaning saddles mostly. He did Western saddles for one dollar and English ones for twenty-five cents. He made more money on Western saddles because it didn't take four times as long to clean one.

"You got time for six?" Fonz asked.

"Sure."

Then Fonz stood back and took a look at Blue. "You got the wrong tack on this horse," he said. "Looks like a stock horse to me. Ever try any rollbacks with him? Sliding stops? Or maybe a cuttin' horse. With hocks like that he ought to be real handy. Got any cow sense?"

"Nope," JoBob said, figuring that would answer all of Fonz's questions. "He's a hunter. Maybe a jumper. Hocks like his are good for a jumper too, you know."

"Hee, hee." Fonz was giggling almost as bad as the girls at school. JoBob was sure tired of people making cracks about Blue's looks.

"You watch him," he said. "You'll see."

When they got to the ring Slim was standing in the middle by the schooling fences talking to Red Baxter. While they hacked around the ring JoBob glanced over at Red and Slim every now and then. They were deep in conversation, and JoBob figured that they were involved in some sort of negotiation. Either Red was trying to sell a horse to Slim, or Slim was trying to sell one to Red. Or maybe it was more complicated than that. They could be talking trades—three or four horses, future possibilities. When Slim started dealing, there was no telling what he would do, and usually the more complicated it was, the better he liked it.

But then Red walked out of the ring, heading up to the barns, and Slim turned his attention to the three of them. He set some jumps and everything else went out of JoBob's head. This was serious. He tightened his legs and talked to Blue through the reins, adjusting his stride, supporting him around the turns, making sure that he got to the fences right. By the time they were done Slim had jacked up the oxer to about four feet and JoBob really started to enjoy himself. The little fences were so easy for Blue that sometimes he got sloppy. But four foot was big enough to catch his attention, and when he was attuned like that it was wonderful.

Sometimes JoBob dreamed that he could fly. In some dreams he could only fly low, barely flittering over the ground like a little swallow, but other times he could take off like an eagle—dive from the heights, plummeting toward the earth, then level out and sail along over fields of alfalfa and corn and cotton, cruise effortlessly through the air over housetops and steeples and office buildings, then abandon the earth altogether, take off and soar high, high up into the sky, free and easy with no limits at all. . . . Jumping Blue was as blissful as those dreams, and tomorrow, when the show started, it was going to be better than a dream. It was going to be *real*.

9
■■■

T HE NEXT MORNING JoBob was up at dawn. He did his chores, thinking not about them, but about what he'd *really* come to the show for. To show Blue. To see how he was going to measure up in competition. He was showing Blue and Twinkle in the Junior Working Hunter division—one class each day—where the horse would be judged. He was also riding Blue in the medal classes, where the rider would be judged. K.T. complained about riding in the medal classes. He said he didn't care what he looked like and judging *his* form was silly. He could get the horse over the fence, and *that's* what counted. But Slim said "form follows function" and at home he made them ride without stirrups and do what they called "the Fort Riley exercises." They rode on the flat precisely one horse-length apart while they worked at the gaits Slim called out: collected trot and extended, leg yields diagonally across the ring, and so on. Slim could think of lots of things. JoBob enjoyed these exercises. He could feel the difference in the way Blue performed, and if they were good enough for the cavalry at Fort Riley, he figured they were good enough for him.

JoBob got through the first few hours of the morning by keeping busy. Then it was time for Junior Working Hunters and JoBob went to get Blue ready. When Blue was tacked up, JoBob looped the reins over his neck and stood off to look at him, cautioning him with his hand to stand still. JoBob had taught him to stand on command and when he gave the signal, Blue stood. Even if he were within sight of something appetizing like a flake of hay or a patch of green grass, he wouldn't move. Earlier that morning JoBob had given him a bath and now he sparkled all over. All his white parts—his socks and blaze and the splotches on his body—were a dazzling white and the chestnut parts glinted in the sun. His mane was neatly braided and his tail so clean it wisped like silk. He was turned out like a hunter, at any rate.

"Okay," JoBob said, "this is important, hear?" Blue raised his head and curled his upper lip up, exposing his teeth in what looked like a grin. Then he lowered his head and looked at JoBob with both ears forward, as if he were saying, "Sure I know it's important, but let's keep this in perspective. It's going to be fun, too." Some horses were smarter than others, just like people, but Blue was the first horse JoBob had met that he could really talk to—that *understood*. He even talked back. "No playing around today," JoBob said. "We're going to show K.T. and Fonz and everybody else what you can do. Okay?" Blue gave a soft whinny of acknowledgment. "All right!" JoBob said, "let's go!" Then he swung into the saddle and headed for the ring.

Before he got on, JoBob had looked at the course diagram, which was posted by the ring. He'd memorized the sequence of fences and turns. It didn't have any big problems, just a couple of small ones that he knew Blue could handle. As he walked up to the ring JoBob thought about how he would ride the course. It was set for a slightly shorter stride than Blue's natural one, so he'd start out with a nice slow collected canter and tick right around, keeping it even and smooth.

When he got to the schooling ring only a few other riders had showed up. Besides K.T. and Trumaine, there were the Blackstone sisters, Tracy and Celia, with their trainer, Ted Huggles, standing in the middle of the ring beside Slim. Tracy and Celia were both real good riders and they always had nice horses. Today Tracy was riding Rambling Rose, a big reliable bay mare that she'd won a lot with last year. And Celia was on a dark dapple gray with a white tail that JoBob had never seen before. He was pretty enough to be in the conformation division and was a real good mover. Knowing the kind of horses the Blackstones had, JoBob was sure he'd be a good jumper too. JoBob had been cool as a cucumber all morning long. Now his stomach started fluttering around as if it had been invaded by a flock of starlings. Then he spotted Sylvia Spencer approaching the warm-up ring, and his stomach got worse. She was so good she'd gone back East to the medal finals last year—and had ended up in the top ten. He was just a fifteen-year-old kid on an ex-lesson horse. What the *hell* was he doing here?

JoBob sighed and sent Blue into the trot. As long as he *was* here, he might as well do the best he could. He was thankful that the schooling ring wasn't crowded yet—it would give him some room to do the Fort Riley exercises.

After he'd trotted once around the schooling ring, JoBob was ready to go back to the barn. He'd been counting on Blue and Blue was no longer acting like the sane, sensible horse he usually was. He stuck his head straight up in the air like a giraffe; he spooked at the balloons tied by the concessions stand; he shied at dogs frisking in the grass outside the ring. Then a trailer pulled up on the road between the schooling ring and the main ring. One of the horses inside kicked and smashed at the sides, the steel shoes clattering on the metal sides of the trailer as loud as a jackhammer. The trailer rocked dangerously, the driver jumped out of the truck yelling, "Whoa! Whoa!" Other people came running and yelling while the horses in the trailer kept right on kicking. Blue squealed and bolted. He was halfway around the ring before JoBob had him under control again. He brought him to a halt and made him stand, noticing that all the other horses were warming up, unphased by all the commotion. He also noticed Celia Blackstone's gray horse jumping the oxer. JoBob had guessed right; he was a lovely jumper.

"Settle down," JoBob told Blue. "This will *not* do." Blue flicked his ears back. "All right," JoBob said. "That's more like it. Never mind all this other stuff. You pay attention to *me.*"

He set off at the trot again, sitting deep in the

saddle and working the bit to get him collected. Blue trotted on, his ears swiveling back toward JoBob. JoBob rode him in circles and half-turns, leg-yielding from the center back over to the rail. JoBob sighed with relief. This was more like it. All this while Slim, with arms folded, had been standing in the middle of the ring next to the schooling jumps along with Ted Huggles, the Blackstones' trainer, and a couple of other trainers. JoBob knew that Slim was watching Blue turn into a fruitcake while JoBob was trying to get organized; but everything had happened so fast there wasn't time to talk. Once the commotion had subsided, and JoBob had Blue back to behaving like a normal horse, Slim unfolded his arms, walked over to one of the schooling fences, and made it into a crossrail.

"He looks like he's settled down, now," Slim said. "You ready to trot this X?"

"I'm ready," JoBob said.

As soon as they started jumping, JoBob felt even better. Nothing got Blue's attention the way jumping did. After they'd trotted back and forth over the X a few times, Slim had them canter the vertical, and then the oxer. They jumped each one several times—not so many that the horses got tired or bored, but enough so their jumping muscles were loosened up and their eye was in gear.

"Okay," Slim said, "let's go with that."

JoBob and K.T. and Trumaine walked over to the ring and stood waiting while the awards for the previous class were being presented. Fonz Robertson was standing by the rail along with Red Baxter and Irma. "Hey,

94

JoBob," he said. "You got here one class too soon. Cow ponies are the *next* class. Hee, hee."

"You watch," JoBob said. "You'll see what he can do."

K.T. laughed too. "We'll see, all right."

JoBob was really steaming. He wanted to kill K.T. and Fonz. Why did Fonz have to choose this minute, right before JoBob was going into the ring, to give K.T. another chance to rub it in? But, he decided, trying to calm down, it was his *last* chance. He'd show K.T. And everybody else too. They wouldn't think it was so funny when Blue got pinned right up there with all the fancy Thoroughbreds like Charlie.

"Okay, Blue," he whispered. "This is it!"

But Fonz and K.T. had rattled JoBob; and Blue knew it. He tossed his head and jigged and pranced. JoBob tried to settle him back to a walk, but Blue was bouncing around like a bobber on a fishline.

The gateman called, "Number fifty-nine? JoBob?"

"Right here," JoBob said, jigging up to the gate.

The gateman swung the gate open. "Let's *go!*"

JoBob headed in the gate hoping that when Blue saw the fences he'd concentrate on them and forget about being nervous. Hoping that somehow *he'd* stop being nervous. "The rider maketh the horse," after all. It was up to him.

The best way to start a hunter course was to trot part of a circle, then pick up the canter and establish the right pace for the rest of the course. In Blue's frame of mind JoBob was sure he'd trot like a Hackney pony with too much knee action and his head up in the stargazing position, not long and low the way a hunter ought to go. He decided to forget the trot, gave Blue a canter signal, and hoped it would do the trick. He *had* to settle him down by the time he got to the first fence. Blue was long-strided enough as it was, and if he didn't calm down his whole plan was shot to hell in a handbasket—they'd eat the distances, get too deep to the last fences in the lines, run through the spots to the single fences and . . .

JoBob cantered along the rail in front of the grandstand. Halfway down the rail he planned to turn and head back through the center of the ring in the direction of the first fence. The first fence was a brush and they'd be jumping going toward the gate. All horses knew where the gate was and jumped more boldly in that direction. That was usually an advantage, especially for the first fence, but in Blue's frame of mind, it wasn't. Going past the grandstand Blue bowed out, half-shying in an attempt to get as far away from the crowd and the noise as he could. JoBob ignored these antics, and halfway down the rail he turned left and headed through the middle of the ring back toward the brush fence. Blue was galloping almost flat-out, much too fast and pulling like a locomotive. JoBob tried to get him down to a decent pace, but Blue wasn't responding and the fence was coming up fast. Too fast. "Blue," JoBob said, *"please."* Then he saw the spot where they ought to take off for the fence, but Blue was tearing toward it at the same too-fast pace. They were going to be dead wrong. JoBob was in despair, but he'd tried; and now it was too late. Blue jumped the fence—somehow—but he hit it hard and didn't use his shoulder at all. What a mess!

That did it, though. Blue hated hitting fences and that brought him to his senses. JoBob too. Here he was in a situation he could control and he was on the verge of bailing out. He sat deep in the saddle and thought: settle, settle, settle. And he did. Blue cantered around the turn and headed for the first line feeling almost like his normal self. They jumped the first fence of the line nice and round and JoBob breathed an enormous sigh of relief. Now it was going to be all right. They cantered on down to the next fence and it worked out just fine. Good! They were clicking now.

They jumped on through the rest of the course with no problems and finished up with a circle. JoBob dropped back to a sitting trot and went on out the gate.

Slim and Irma were standing along the back rail, a few yards past the gate, with several other trainers. K.T. was heading in the gate and Trumaine was walking Lulu back and forth, getting ready to go in the ring after K.T. Slim made a circle with his thumb and forefinger, then tilted his head toward the ring where K.T. and Charlie were cantering their warm-up circle.

JoBob wanted to talk to Slim, but he had to wait until Trumaine and K.T. had finished their rounds. K.T. on Charlie put in one of their typical smooth, polished trips. Lulu and Trumaine were another story. Lulu cantered up to the first fence and came to a screeching halt. Trumaine sailed over her head and landed on his rear end on the other side of the fence.

"You need to jump the fence with the horse too," someone yelled from the rail.

Trumaine got up, brushed the dirt off his breeches and led Lulu out of the ring, a spot of red on each cheek.

"How many times do I have to tell you?" Slim asked. "You gotta get your engine revved. She needs some gas to get around the course, boy."

"I know," Trumaine said, "but . . ."

"He was trying," Irma said. "You all right, Trumaine?"

"Yeah," Trumaine muttered. "I'll get her going next time."

"You do that," Slim said. "Maybe you can borrow some juice from JoBob and Blue. It's not a steeplechase in there, JoBob. You got to get some control going toward the gate. That first fence was a mess."

"I know," JoBob said, "but I was rattled. K.T.—"

"K.T. what?"

"Nothin'."

Slim gave him a hard look. "When you're in the ring ain't nobody with you. Unless you take them in your head."

"Yeah, I know."

"Well, it was a good trip except for that first fence. You'll get it."

Then Slim turned to talk to K.T.

"That was great, Joseph R.!" Trumaine said.

"You see the first fence?" JoBob asked. "It was a disaster."

Trumaine shrugged. "You see mine? I thought you were real good for the first class."

JoBob jumped off and ran up his stirrups. That was just like Trumaine. Shrugging off his own mistakes, then looking at the bright side.

"He's right, JoBob," Irma said. "This was just the first class. The first *day*. There are other classes. It'll be all right."

"I guess," JoBob said. But he was disappointed. He'd wanted so bad to make a good first impression.

"Nice go," he said to K.T.

"Thanks," K.T. said, with a smug look. "You were pretty good too. Too bad you blew the first fence."

JoBob handed Blue to Irma and went to get on Twinkle. She had a pretty good round, considering how green she was. Not good enough for a ribbon, JoBob didn't think, but he was satisfied. At least she hadn't come unglued like Blue had.

The loudspeaker crackled and JoBob listened to the announcer call out the numbers and names of the people who placed. Celia Blackstone won it on her pretty gray horse, who was named South Coast, and K.T. on Charlie was second. JoBob didn't wait around to watch the presentation of awards.

When he got back to the barn, JoBob put Twinkle away. Then he untacked Blue and turned him loose in his stall. Blue went to the back corner and stood with his head down and ears flopping. He looked ashamed.

JoBob went inside and stroked his neck. "Blue, I'm sorry. But Irma's right. That was just the first class. We've got a medal class this afternoon and another hunter class tomorrow. I *promise* not to lose my cool. Give you a fighting chance, okay?"

He waited for a sign from Blue, but Blue just stood there. Then he heaved a sigh and walked over to his water bucket. When he raised his head from the bucket, he looked at JoBob again and this time he looked reproachful. "Tell you what, though," JoBob said in a voice so low it was almost a whisper. "I need your help too. No more coming unglued in the schooling ring, okay?" Blue's ears pricked forward as if he was listening hard; then he stepped close to JoBob. "We're in this together," JoBob went on, "and it's not just to show those other people. It's really for us, right?" Blue touched JoBob's cheek with his nose and JoBob rubbed Blue gently behind his ears, positive that Blue understood this time. He understood it himself, in a way that he hadn't before.

10

...

ALL DAY LONG on Friday while JoBob was bustling around, back in the edges of his mind he was thinking about the afternoon when he'd be riding Blue in working hunters. He'd be forking straw into the wheelbarrow, or taking Samantha up to the ring for Irma, or topping off water buckets, and he'd feel the spice of anticipation. We'll tick right around, he told himself, just like we did in the medal class yesterday. Blue was really good in that class. No reason why we can't do it again.

Blue had been solid in that class. He hadn't bounced around outside the gate, and when they were in the ring, he concentrated on the fences. He responded to JoBob's aids. They wound up third, and that made JoBob happy. It was a big class with some real good riders in it—people like Sylvia Spencer and the Blackstone sisters. But it was a medal class, where the rider was judged. JoBob still wished that it had been Blue who had won the ribbon, not him.

GODLEY MIDDLE SCHOOL LIBRARY

101

No horse show day ever dragged, but this one came close. Then, when the sun was already lowering down in the west and the evening chill was stealing through the fairgrounds, the announcer's voice called, "Okay you juniors! Thirty minutes until the working hunters. Let's start gettin' 'em ready!"

JoBob went into Blue's stall and stood quietly, looking at him for a long time. His horse. "All right, Blue," he said, "this is it. Think you can do it?"

Blue whuffled JoBob's hair and made little chomping noises with his teeth, never actually taking a bite—he just liked to play at it. "Okay," JoBob said, taking the soft brush from the grooming box, "time to get serious. I want you to be as good as you were in the medal yesterday, because this time *you* will be judged." He went all over Blue carefully, then he tacked him up and led him outside where the light was better. He swabbed at a manure stain on his hock with alcohol, and then went over the rest of his coat with the damp rub rag to pick up any bits of dust he'd missed with the soft brush. Then there was nothing more to do. It was time.

In the schooling ring he settled into the rhythm of Blue's trot, then the rocking three-beat rhythm of the canter, and finally the pure soaring joy of the jumps. Blue felt better than he ever had: he was awake and keen, responding instantly to JoBob's aids, utterly concentrated, not one bit stiff or nervous.

"Okay," Slim said to K.T. and Trumaine and JoBob when they'd finished the warm-up routine. "You all go on over to the ring and we'll talk about the course."

The three of them gathered by the rail near the

102

back gate with Slim at the center of their cluster.

"Now what do you all think about this course?" he asked.

"Looks pretty straightforward," K.T. said.

"I reckon it is," Slim said. "Just be sure you have enough pace, Trumaine. And you be sure you don't have too much, JoBob. And you just ride like you know how, K.T. This course is so simple that *everything* will count."

At that moment Tony, the gateman, called, "Number fifty-eight? K.T. and Dealer's Choice? You're in the hole!"

K.T. moved off at the walk so Charlie wouldn't be stiff from standing when he went into the ring, and JoBob and Trumaine fell in behind him. They'd all put their numbers in together, so they'd be going in the ring directly after K.T.

"Good luck," Trumaine said.

"You too," JoBob said.

Trumaine grinned. "Just hope I don't land flat on my ass, like I did yesterday."

"You'll be all right," JoBob said, though he wasn't so sure about that. Then he stood in his stirrups, pushing his weight down into his heels, while he walked Blue back and forth in the space behind the back gate. He didn't stop to watch K.T. He wanted to concentrate on his own job. Slim was right. On a simple course like this, even a tiny mistake would be obvious. If he got his shoulders forward or his legs a fraction too tight, Blue would get on too long a stride and the distances would be wrong. Or if JoBob got tense, Blue would feel it and he might start playing

103

around. He might buck or shy, or . . . By the time Tony called, "Okay, Number fifty-nine! JoBob? You're in the hole!" he'd thought of ninety-nine things that could go wrong. This will not do, he told himself. He made his body relax and started erasing all the negative pictures from his mind, getting it instead to produce a picture of the course the way it ought to be ridden.

"JoBob!" Tony called from the gate. "You're on deck!"

No more time for worrying or thinking. Time now to do it. The gate opened and JoBob was in the ring. He did a nice collected trot for half of the warm-up circle, then he set Blue into a canter, getting it to match the one he'd had in his mind. Blue was both relaxed and alert. Perfect. They cantered down to the first fence, and jumped it just fine. JoBob was even more confident now. He relaxed into Blue, feeling the harmony of the two of them together. Every fence was going to be as good as that one, he knew it. They were on a roll now. They went on around the course keeping the right lick, meeting every fence right in stride.

Then they were over the last fence. JoBob was elated. It was as good as they could do, he knew. He wanted to whoop and holler, dance a jig, or let rip with a rebel yell. But he was still in the ring. You couldn't carry on like that while you were in the ring. So he cantered a finishing circle, remembering to keep Blue bent correctly. Then he sank into the saddle and headed for the gate at a sitting trot.

Loud clapping and cheering sounded from the grandstand.

"Very nice!" Irma said, as soon as he was out the gate.

"Thanks," JoBob said, smiling, in the midst of the flurry of dismounting from Blue, running up the stirrups, and transferring his saddle to Twinkle.

"That was well done," Slim said.

"Sure was," Trumaine echoed, grinning from ear to ear.

Slim did one of his hat adjustments. Gave the brim a final pat and said it again. "Well done." Even though JoBob had thought they were pretty good and even though he'd heard Trumaine and Irma say it, having Slim confirm it convinced him. Irma and Trumaine were always positive, but Slim wasn't.

JoBob was feeling silly-happy. He raised his right hand like a Comanche signaling "How!," grinning a challenge at Trumaine. Trumaine raised his hand too, and their hands met with a satisfying, affirming thwack.

"How was K.T.?" JoBob asked Trumaine.

"Same as usual," Trumaine answered. "Just about perf," and JoBob thought, why can't he do something wrong, just once? Then he asked Trumaine how he had been, and Trumaine grinned. "I got around. Jumped every fence, *with* my horse."

"All right!" They slapped hands again, then JoBob had to get busy with Twinkle. He got on Twinkle and went over to the warm-up ring. While he was schooling her he decided he was glad K.T. had done well. That meant that if he and Blue placed over them, K.T. wouldn't have any excuse.

Then he stopped thinking about all that and made himself concentrate on Twinkle. He owed it to Slim to give her as good a ride as he could. She'd been pretty good the day before, jumped better than she ever had at home, and JoBob wanted her to be at least that good today too. She was.

Then there was the usual milling and stirring around that happened when a class was over. The loudspeaker crackled and the announcer started talking to himself—at least JoBob figured that's what he was doing—repeating the class specifications for what must have been the tenth time that day, so why would anyone listen? Then, at last, his voice swung from the singsong of reading the class specifications into a higher pitch, like an auctioneer singing out "Sold!": "In first place is Number fifty-nine, Blue Chip, owned and ridden by Mr. Joseph Draper. . . ."

First! JoBob ran in the gate with Blue's reins in his hand. Blue threw up his head and capered along beside him. JoBob ran a little faster, trying to run off some of the happiness. Blue squealed and bucked, as if he knew that he'd done something to be proud of. JoBob jogged down the center of the ring, past the jumps flanked with flowers, past the crowd in the grandstand and the judge sitting alone on the top seat, JoBob's feet and Blue's moving soundlessly over the springy tanbark with no one in front of him. No one at all. No thing either, except a swift bright vision of the future: the classes they had left at this show on Saturday and Sunday. Then the show in Yreka only a few weeks away, and the summer shows where they'd range farther afield—down south to Bakersfield and Del Mar and Monterey. He and Blue would be doing a lot more of this. On and on they'd go, easy as riffs of wind over a field of winter wheat.

106

Oh yes, JoBob thought. We'll go; we'll do it. This is just the first taste of honey.

When he came out of the ring people called "Congratulations!" from all sides. "That little horse can jump, all right," Fonz said. "Well done!" Irma smiled. "What'd I tell you about old Yance," Slim said with a nod of satisfaction.

JoBob smiled and smiled. He said thanks to all the people along the rail, and stole a minute to whisper thanks and congratulations to Blue too. Then he hung the blue ribbon on Blue's bridle, tucked the silver tray under his arm, and turned to watch the others coming out of the ring. Sylvia Spencer cocked her head and gave him a thumbs-up. Celia Blackstone smiled, "Good ride!" K.T. nodded at JoBob and muttered, "Pretty good, JoBob."

JoBob said, "Thanks," pretending that K.T. had really meant it.

Back at the barn they hung their ribbons on the wire above the tack room and then took their horses down to their stalls. "You did great," JoBob told Blue. "And you did understand how important it was for us, didn't you?" Blue nuzzled his hair. "Sure you do," JoBob said, "and I'm glad. Do it again tomorrow?" Blue nuzzled him again and JoBob finished, "Sure we will. Blue ribbons match your name, and they look real nice."

JoBob set the silver tray on the table in the tack room, running his finger around the fancy border, which was crimped like a pie crust. He'd won lots of trophies with Slim's horses that he'd showed last year and the year before. Technically, the trophy belonged to the owner of the horse, but Slim said he didn't have any use for candy dishes or flower vases, and JoBob had done most of the work, so he ought to have them. JoBob didn't have much use for them either. He hung the ribbons on a string in his room and gave the trophies to his mother. She said they were nice, then stuck them in a kitchen cabinet where JoBob noticed them every now and then, getting tarnished because no one polished them. This tray was different from all those others. It was *really* his, and Blue's, and JoBob thought it was the prettiest thing he'd ever seen.

Then it was time to get busy with the rest of his end-of-the-day chores. All around them people were closing their horses' stall doors, locking tack rooms, and starting up their trucks and heading out of the fairgrounds. The bustle of the day tailed off with the sun, and the rhythm settled into evening.

When they'd finished their chores, JoBob and Trumaine rolled out their bedrolls in the tack room. At least JoBob did. Trumaine had a new sleeping bag like JoBob had never seen before. It had dark green canvas on the outside and a red plaid flannel lining on the inside with some kind of padding in between and a zipper along the side and bottom. JoBob stretched out in his bedroll and Trumaine zipped up his sleeping bag. From outside they could hear two girls talking, their voices a low murmur like leaves in the woods; and from the next aisle an occasional sharp swearword or yelp of glee came from the grooms who were in the midst of their evening crap game. Then all the dogs on the grounds tuned up and yowled, mournful as coyotes, at a siren in the distance.

It had been a good day. It was going to be a good show, JoBob could feel it in his bones. It was going to be a good *year*: him and Blue clicking around course after course, just like they'd done today, sailing over fence after fence, and no one ever again was going to make cracks about Blue's looks. He'd proved what he could do. Everyone admitted it. Except K.T.

All of a sudden JoBob realized what he'd just said to himself: *everyone admitted it*. Including the judge. So what did he care about K.T.? If he wanted to be sour grapes about it, let him. JoBob was having a wonderful time. No sense in letting K.T. spoil it.

JoBob sighed down into his bedroll. The girls' laughter sounded through the night, light and silvery as the tinkly bells of sheep echoing high up in a mountain pasture. They reminded him of Mariko. She didn't even know that he was going to this show. He wondered if she wondered where he was. Then he decided that didn't matter. *He* wondered where *she* was. He tried to picture her. Right now he supposed she'd be somewhere in her house. But that was too hard. He could only picture her in the places he'd seen her: waiting for the bus, in class at school, in the cafeteria; but those were like old faded photographs. What he *saw* was her out in the woods with her mushroom basket in her hand and the shadows of the trees playing across her hair. Her eyes dark and solemn. What he heard was, "Was that your horse I saw you riding the other day? The pretty brown with the white spots?"

He wished he'd said, "Sure," instead of all that stuff about her spying on him and that you don't call horses brown. He decided that when he got home on Sunday evening he'd go over to her house and ask her if she wanted to go mushrooming after school the next day. In all the years they'd lived down the road from each other he'd never gone over to her house and knocked on the door. It would be a strange and unusual thing to do, and JoBob wondered if he would actually be able to do it.

Well, why not? This was the year for strange and unusual things.

11

■ ■ ■

Being at a horse show was like being plopped in the middle of a days-long carnival. JoBob loved it all—the sights and sounds and smells, the ups and downs of competition, the hurly-burly atmosphere that started before dawn and lasted into the evening, the vapor coming out of the horses' nostrils when he went to feed them in the morning, wraiths of white that puffed when he opened the doors of their stalls and curled on out into the morning air mingling with the gray-white of the thick tule fog off the river bottom. He liked the warm yeasty smell inside the stalls, and the slight astringency of saddle soap, and the whiffs of mustard and hot dogs that drifted down from the concessions stand. As the day progressed there was a parade of grooms and riders going up to the ring and coming back; and there was the action in the ring itself along with the sideshows happening along the way in the barn aisles, the grandstand, over at the schooling ring, and the concessions stand. One of the things JoBob noticed was K.T. hanging around with Sylvia Spencer, talking so intently they might have been the only two people in the whole world. He also noticed Slim and Ted Huggles, the Blackstones' trainer, deep in conversation a couple of times. Talking some kind of a deal, JoBob supposed. All sorts of things went on at horse shows besides the horse show.

When JoBob didn't have a class to ride in or a horse to get ready for one he'd leave his barn work for later and snatch some time up at the ring with Trumaine and Irma. They'd park themselves in the grandstand and settle into the subtle beauty of a hunter class, where all the colors were soft as old tweeds in an English fog, or sit up on the edge of their seats yelling encouragement as a rider streaked for time in a jumper class, turning faster than a horse ought to be able to turn and jumping a solid, scary-looking yellow and black panel with only two strides to calculate the distance. The stock horses got them up on the edges of their seats too—the way they galloped flat-out down the center of the ring and came to a sliding stop with their haunches so far under them they looked like cougars coiled to spring; then, quick as cats too, they whirled into spins and rollbacks. Then there were high-stepping Hackney ponies and the five-gaited Saddlebreds, who came into the ring with their heads up, manes flying, and tails streaking behind them like banners, popping their knees higher than a jumper over the top of a fence. JoBob and Trumaine and Irma, too, rattled their feet on the floorboards of the grandstand and whooped out rebel yells along with the grooms and handlers along the rail when the call came to "Rack on!" JoBob figured that Irma was about as old as his mother, but she sure didn't act like it.

You could always learn by watching. JoBob had learned a lot, but you never knew it all. From the Saddlebred riders he learned about showmanship— how to come in the ring and command attention by being flashier than every other horse and rider in the ring. To make passes in front of the judge whenever possible, and to stay on show as long as you were in the ring, making a final dramatic sweep in your horse's best gait right in front of the judge even after the announcer had called, "Line up! All line up, please!" And in the lineup too. Those gaited riders didn't slump down and hold their reins looped casually in one hand resting on their horse's withers the way some hunter riders did. They sat up with their shoulders back, both hands on the reins and their legs on their horses' sides, ready to move out should they be summoned back to the rail for a workout.

From the Western riders he learned precision. They cultivated an image even more low-key than the hunter riders. They looked super relaxed, like they were just sitting there doing nothing, but JoBob knew better. He knew those horses had years of training behind them, and the riders were cuing them all the time, with things as subtle as a tensed muscle in the right thigh, or a lift of the reins by a quarter of an inch, which the horses responded to instantly.

Of course, he watched most closely in the hunter and jumper classes, especially the jumpers, where the fences were bigger and the courses trickier. Hunter courses were set for a horse's natural stride and designed to be ridden smoothly, but jumper courses were designed with problems and to ride such a course well required great accuracy and ability. Plus guts.

JoBob had it in the back of his mind to ride Blue in jumpers—maybe next year after he'd had a year of experience as a hunter. There was no rush. So he sat up and paid close attention when it was time for jumpers.

"I can't wait until I can ride Blue in jumpers," he said to Trumaine. "It'll be a lot more fun than hunters."

"Try to get over that big black and yellow thing?" Trumaine asked, nodding at one of the jumps. "Never catch me doing that."

"You're not even tempted?"

Trumaine smiled and shrugged. "What for? Lulu doesn't have the personality to be a jumper. Too lazy."

"And neither do I," he added after a minute. "Hunter fences are plenty high enough for me."

JoBob didn't say anything. Trumaine was right, he knew. He was too easygoing to tackle something as strenuous and difficult as jumpers, but it was hard to *really* understand how he could be so lackadaisical.

As usual, Trumaine looked relaxed as he leaned against the back of the bleachers with one leg crossed over the other and his hands folded across his stomach. All of a sudden JoBob felt uncomfortable and uneasy, the way he felt when he was with his father. JoBob told himself he was being silly, but the feeling lingered. After a few minutes he understood what it was. Trumaine *was* like his father in one essential way: he

114

had no hustle. JoBob wasn't going to live his life like a passenger, just letting things happen, the way Trumaine rode, while someone else made the important decisions and did the real work. If he did that he'd end up like his father—sitting around and dreaming up schemes that never worked out, living off his wife and a tenant. No pride at all. No get-up-and-go either.

JoBob loved to watch, but he had a lot of work to do, too—grooming, mucking, cleaning tack, showing Twinkle to potential buyers. The best part, of course, was showing Blue, and often in the midst of his other activities JoBob would see himself and Blue in the ring. He'd see himself picking up the silver tray and the blue ribbon, tipping his hat to the trophy lady, or he'd think about the next class they were going to ride in and get excited way ahead of time.

On Saturday morning they placed fourth in hunters. K.T. was third and after the class he'd said, "Good ride," to JoBob, sounding almost friendly.

"Well, thanks," JoBob said with a smile. He wondered if K.T. was being friendly because he and Charlie had just placed over him and Blue, or because JoBob had decided he really didn't care what K.T. thought. And K.T. somehow knew how JoBob felt, so he wasn't going to play that little game anymore. All of a sudden he remembered what Slim had said about thinking, being smart. That's what he'd done—almost without realizing it. And it had worked. Apparently.

In the Maclay medal class in the afternoon, K.T. was first to go. After he'd ridden, he came over to

JoBob and gave him a couple of pointers about how to ride the course. JoBob thought about it for a long time, wondering if K.T. was telling the truth. So he watched several other people ride the course and decided that K.T. was being straight, wasn't trying to trip him up. He followed his advice and wound up second. K.T. was out of the ribbons, and JoBob figured he'd turn snotty again. But he went up to K.T.— just to see.

"Thanks a lot, K.T.," JoBob said. "That was real helpful advice."

"Any time," K.T. said. "You did the riding and it was a real hard course."

Funny, JoBob thought, how sometimes when you let go of something, it just dropped into your lap.

The Maclay was JoBob's last class that day, and when it was over it was still pretty early. JoBob did all his work at Slim's barn and then hustled over to Fonz's to clean saddles for him. While he was soaping a saddle he thought about the classes he was going to ride in the next day—the Junior Working Hunter Stake and Bareback Equitation. He figured the Bareback Eq would be a piece of cake. He didn't think many folks at the show had jumped as many fences bareback as he and Blue had. *And* they had a shot at Reserve Champion in working hunters. To be winning ribbons at all in that kind of company was nothing to be sniffed at, and JoBob was really pleased. But Reserve Champion! That would mean that Blue was the second best horse in their division.

Only one more day of the show left, JoBob thought,

feeling sad already. It had gone much too fast. Oh well, he told himself, school would be out in another month and he had the whole summer ahead of him. Long, lazy days he could spend at the barn without any schoolwork to interfere. And then, after the Siskiyou County Fair up in Yreka, in June, they'd head down south for the A circuit. Three, four shows in a row. They'd have a ball.

While JoBob was putting away Fonz's last saddle, his stomach growled and he remembered that Irma was over at their barn cooking up a barbeque. He was tired and he was hungry. Any kind of nourishment would be welcome, but Irma's food was something special. He said good night to Fonz and headed for their barn walking fast. Two aisles away he caught a whiff of the charcoal smoke and the chicken sizzling on the grate, and he almost ran, it smelled so good.

In front of the tack room they'd set up a table and Irma had covered it with a red and white checked tablecloth and set some primroses in a glass jar in the middle. On the ground beside the table were a picnic hamper and an ice chest. Irma flew back and forth between the grill and the table. At the grill she stood beside Slim, who'd been delegated to cook the chicken.

"Now you watch that chicken, Slim," she said. "It'll burn if you don't keep your eye on it."

"Yes, ma'am," Slim said, rolling his eyes. "I can tend to a few little birds. Shoot, did I ever tell you about the way we used to do turkeys back home?"

On her way back to the table, Irma called "Yep" over her shoulder.

GODLEY MIDDLE SCHOOL LIBRARY

"Well," Slim went on, for all the world as if she'd said "Nope." "We'd dig us a pit 'bout three foot deep and just as long. One, two feet wide. Line it with stones. And the day beforehand we'd start up a fire—none of this store-bought charcoal in a sack, but a good ol' mesquite fire. Smell of that would make your stomach roar, I'll tell you." He pointed the tongs at Trumaine and JoBob and winked. "And keep her stoked up until the stones are red-hot. Then you let her die down and bank it with grass, put in your turkeys, or your antelopes, or your deer, cover 'em with more grass and hot stones on top. Then you seal her up. Next day you've got the tastiest, tenderest eatin' you ever even dreamed of."

Back in front of the tack room Irma took bowls of deviled eggs and potato salad and baked beans from the hamper and set them on the table. "You watch out, Slim," she called. "I smell something burning."

"Just a little piece of wing," Slim said. "They oughta redesign chickens so their wings ain't so little and don't stick out so much."

"Here, Trumaine," Irma said. "Take this sauce and give him a hand. Ladle it over every piece and spread them onto the edges of the fire or else we'll be having cinders for dinner."

Half the dogs on the show grounds appeared out of nowhere, tongues lolling. "Go on," Slim yelled. "Scat!" They'd slink back a few paces and linger just out of kicking range. When Slim wasn't watching they'd start edging forward again.

"Sure smells good," JoBob said.

"Glad somebody appreciates it," Irma said, good

118

and loud so Slim could hear it. "Real chicken's better than a Texas tall tale. Stick to your ribs at least."

"I'm not complaining," Slim said. "You can't ride worth spit, but you sure can cook."

"Button it up, Mr. Abbott," she said. "Keep on talking like that, I might decide to take my talents elsewhere." She was smiling, though.

Slim was right. She was a good cook. He was also right about her riding. She rode the old-fashioned way, with long stirrups and her butt way back in the saddle. Slim told her that no one rode like that anymore except a few old fogeys over in England who'd never heard of Caprilli or the forward seat. "And me," Irma said. "I've been riding like this my whole life long. Too old to change now." Irma wasn't exactly old, but she was pretty old to go falling off all the time. Because sitting back in the saddle the way Irma did, she'd whack Samantha in the kidneys over just about every jump, and jab her in the mouth. Samantha would take it for one, two, sometimes even six or seven fences. Then she'd slam on the brakes and dump Irma into a fence. Irma's form was terrible, but she was gutsy, JoBob had to admit. If he'd been dumped in the middle of a big oxer he wasn't so sure he'd be overjoyed to get back on and try it again. But Irma would get back on, give Samantha a good whack with her crop, and have at it. If it kept happening to him, he thought he'd take up something tamer like golf—not nearly as exciting, but there wasn't much chance of getting your bones broken either. It was nice having her around the shows, though. Even though JoBob was her groom for the show, she helped him too, in all sorts of ways—like holding Twinkle when he was busy with Blue—and she always had a smile and a kind word for all of them.

JoBob stood by the table feeling hungrier and hungrier as Irma unpacked the hamper. Besides the salad and beans there was lime jello with fruit cocktail and little marshmallows inside. *And* chocolate icebox cookies with chocolate frosting. JoBob took a cookie and popped it in his mouth.

"I saw that, JoBob," Irma said. "Shame on you. You'll ruin your appetite."

"Nothing's going to ruin my appetite," JoBob said.

"Well, it looks like everything's ready," she said. "Where's K.T.?"

Slim shrugged. "Haven't seen him in awhile."

"He's off sparkin' Sylvia Spencer, I bet," JoBob said. " 'Least I saw him goin' off in that direction."

"Reckon he's in lo-o-oove," Trumaine said.

Slim stopped with the tongs in midair. "Is *that* what's the matter with him?"

Trumaine blushed and shrugged. "Aw, I don't know. I just said that."

"Well, it happens to everybody sooner or later," Slim said, "and K.T.'s old enough. Why I was—" He broke off and got a misty look in his eyes, not like he was going to cry or anything idiotic like that, but like he was looking at something real far away that had a lot of sweetness to it, and some sadness too. JoBob was astonished. Slim in love?

"It's not going to happen to us," JoBob said. "Right, T?"

"Right," Trumaine said.

"Sure it will," Slim said. "Ain't no way around it.

Long as you're living and breathing and walking upon the earth. Ain't that right, Irma?"

Irma was heading for the grill with a platter for the chicken. "Sure. And you'll get your heart broken too, likely as not."

"My heart's going to be broken in about two seconds," Trumaine said, "if it doesn't get some food."

"Your stomach needs food, not your heart," JoBob said.

"Heart too," Irma said. "Only a different kind."

"What kind?"

"Oh—love, I guess."

"But you just said it would break your heart."

"No. Being in love might. But that's different from loving. Loving . . ." Now *she* was beginning to look funny and JoBob wondered if she was thinking about her husband, who'd been killed in the war. But Irma pulled out of it too. "This chicken is ready," she said.

"Yahoo!" Trumaine and JoBob said together. "So are we!"

Irma laid the chicken out on the platter, spooned extra sauce over it, and brought it to the table. Slim followed with another platter stacked with sweet corn in the husks that had been roasting over the coals. JoBob and Trumaine spread out a horse blanket to one side of the tack room, then filled their plates and sat down. JoBob sighed with pleasure and dug in. Seemed like he was always hungry these days and Irma's food was *good*. He ate two plates full and several chocolate cookies, then he leaned back against the wall and folded his hands over his stomach, feeling just right.

On the radio Bill Haley and the Comets launched into "Rock Around the Clock"—the guitars twanging, the thrum of the drums, the beat fast and compelling.

Trumaine got up and started jitterbugging, moving his shoulders back and forth, snapping his fingers, his feet quick-stepping on the ground. "Hey, Irma!" he said. "Want to dance?"

"I'm too old for that stuff," she said with a smile. "I'll just watch."

"Where the hell'd you learn that?" Slim asked.

Trumaine was absorbed in the dance and didn't answer. He danced on, hips swaying, feet stomping, his whole body loose and moving with the beat, his eyes half-shut. He no longer looked like friendly teddy-bear Trumaine, but someone more alive and more complicated, a person who was yearning after something that JoBob felt too. Love? Growing up? Long before JoBob could figure that one out the music stopped and the DJ, talking fast and loud, launched into an ad for the Big Red Warehouse.

"You ought to boogie like that on horseback," Slim said.

Trumaine dug his toe into the ground and smiled shyly. "It's different."

"Don't seem so different to me," Slim said. "Takes the same kind of coordination and sense of rhythm."

"Yeah," Trumaine said, "but I never know what Lulu is going to do. She's always surprising me."

"Know what you mean," Irma said wryly.

"But you can count on the music," Trumaine said.

On the radio the ads were over and Jaye P. Morgan crooned:

122

A little love that slowly grows and grows
Not one that comes and goes
That's all I want from you . . .

The clouds piled up high and white in the sky, light cottony fluffs turning crimson at the edges.

A sunny day with hopes up to the sky
A kiss and no goodbye
That's all I want from you . . .

She sang on, her voice sweet and haunting; and the clouds began to glow as if they'd swallowed up the ruby of the sun and had their own shine now. JoBob squinted his eyes up so particular objects blurred into washes of color and the glow of the sky seemed to be throbbing inside him as well. "A little love that slowly grows and grows, not one that comes and goes . . ." That's what JoBob wanted. It would be sweet to be with someone, to have a little love, like it said in the song, slowly growing and growing. . . . But no one was going to break his heart. Slim and Irma were wrong about that.

"Hey, JoBob, look who's here!"

"Huh?" He forced his eyes all the way open and himself upright, so the scene came back into focus: Slim and Irma sitting in the captain's chairs, their feet outstretched, arms dangling loose and relaxed, the ribbons fluttering above the tack room, the table littered with empty plates and pop bottles and chicken bones, Trumaine standing in front of them dancing with his eyes closed while the music lilted into the last chorus. All of that fit. But right there in the middle of it was something that did not.

12
■■■

DARLENE. It was like one of those pictures on the back of a comic book: What's Wrong With This Picture? Usually there were lots of things wrong—rabbits in the treetops, fish in the ground, birds in the mailbox, hats on upside-down—but this time there was just one thing wrong. She looked silly as hell in a tight pink skirt and sweater with a lace collar doo-dadded around her neck, her head cocked to one side so her curled hair swung away from her cheek. Darlene practiced poses at home in front of the mirror. JoBob wondered how long she'd been working on this one. He shut his eyes and decided that when he opened them again she would be gone. She wasn't there, hadn't been there at all.

"JoBob, you gotta come on home with me." No mistaking that voice. She was there, all right.

"Home?" he echoed, thinking how dumb it sounded as soon as he said it. But he wasn't the one who was dumb. She was. "I have classes to ride in tomorrow."

124

She tossed her head, shaking it slightly from side to side, not a "no" but another of the practiced gestures. It made her curls bob fetchingly around her cheeks and she rolled her eyes at Trumaine to see if he was watching. He was. So were Slim and Irma.

JoBob got up and walked down the aisle.

"You come here, JoBob," she yelled. "I've got to talk to you."

JoBob kept walking. He wished he could walk on to a place where Darlene could not follow. But she did follow, right down to the end of the aisle where JoBob turned the corner, out of sight of the group in front of the tack room.

"You have to come home, JoBob," she said.

"What for? I'm at a show. I've got work to do."

"You've got work to do at home."

"Like what?"

"Fight tomorrow and . . ."

JoBob rolled his eyes up. "I *know* there's a fight tomorrow. So what? It's got nothin' to do with me."

"Yes it does. Will you be quiet for a minute and listen? It's an emergency. Chet was in a car accident and broke his leg. He's in the hospital, so you've got to come. Daddy needs you."

"Oh come on," JoBob said. "You're makin' it up."

"I am *not*. Think Daddy would let me take the truck if it wasn't important?"

JoBob hadn't thought about that. He stepped back out into the aisle way to where he could see the cars and trucks parked at the end. Sure enough, she did have their father's truck. And she was right. He never let anyone drive that truck, least of all Darlene. Something dreadful happened to JoBob's stomach and he sank down onto a hay bale, trying to get his mind to work. He had to think. He remembered Chet saying, "We've got a lot at stake this time." And his father talking loud and hearty about how it would be a shoo-in. *What* would be a shoo-in? At the time JoBob had been thinking about the show, and Mariko, and he hadn't paid much attention. But now he started to sweat. They'd been talking about something besides a regular old fight. Something that was going to happen at the fight, maybe. Some kind of a deal they'd cooked up.

"You gotta come, JoBob. Daddy's in the blackest mood I've ever seen. Couple of guys are coming down from Yuba City with some new kind of Peruvian birds that are supposed to be really terrific, but Daddy says his'll beat the daylights out of them, 'cept he's got to have some help and Chet is in the hospital, and you're the only other one he trusts and . . ."

"Will you hush, just for a minute?" JoBob said. "I can't think when you keep yammering."

Darlene went on in the same bossy voice. "There's nothing to think about. Like I told you, this is a big fight. There's going to be fifty people there at least." Then she changed her tack. She came close and her eyes were pleading. "Please, JoBob. He needs you. You owe it to him."

That did it. Something snapped inside of JoBob and he didn't need to try and think it out. He knew what he was going to do. "I don't owe him a damn thing," he said. "And I have work to do here. I'm tied for points with K.T. and Sylvia Spencer. Blue

126

could be Reserve Champion. Think I'm going to up and throw practically a whole year's work out the window because Pop decided to go to some dumb fight?" He got up off the hay bale and turned on the hose.

Darlene shook her head, then whistled low, a kind of "whew," ending on a down note. "Please come. *Please*. I'm scared to go home without you." Her mouth quivered and her voice shook. She wasn't posing any more; she was scared. "What am I going to say?"

"Say I ran away, or you couldn't find me, or . . . anything you want." He started down the row of stalls with the hose, filling up the buckets as he went.

Darlene walked behind him making a noise every now and then, an "ach, ach" in the back of her throat that could have been a cough or a choked sob or an expression of pure disgust.

After he'd filled the third bucket JoBob turned. "Go on, Darlene. Bug out."

"No. I'm not budging without you."

"Then you'll have to wait until tomorrow. Tomorrow *afternoon*. After the show's over. After I've ridden Blue in the last class and shown Twinkle to some people who're interested. After I've packed up and loaded the van. I'm working for Slim and I'm not cuttin' out on him."

"I'm talking about your own kin. What do I care about that old redneck, Slim?"

JoBob whirled. "One more word like that and I'll ram this hose down your throat."

"Oh Jesus." Her face balled up like a baby about to cry.

"Cry if you want. It won't do any good."

Tears rolled down her cheeks. She whimpered and sobbed.

JoBob opened the next stall door and stuck the hose in the bucket. Darlene stood behind him sobbing and gasping. Then she emitted a loud snuffle with some kind of finality to it and walked off down the aisle toward the tack room.

Keep walking, JoBob told her mentally. Just keep on walking. Get in the truck and go home.

But it didn't work. Down at the tack room Darlene was talking to Slim and Irma. It wasn't fair. It was *not* fair for her to come and wreck up the best show he'd ever had. *"Goddamnit!"* JoBob bellowed so loud that Samantha jumped and spooked back to the far corner of her stall, where she stood rolling her eyes at him. "Aw, Sammie, I didn't mean you." He went on, trying to soothe her, but she wouldn't move out of the corner. JoBob shrugged and went on to the next stall. She'd get over it.

He was close enough now to hear what Darlene was saying. Just as bad as he thought. Telling them things she shouldn't. She had no right. It was his life.

He went down to the end of the aisle and turned off the hose and coiled it precisely, laying each round exactly on top of the one beneath it. Then he turned and marched down to the tack room. "Okay, Darlene, let's go." He grabbed her arm and started walking toward the truck.

"You mean you're coming?" Her eyes were big and wide and she flashed him her best smile. "What about your stuff?"

"They'll bring it, right, Trumaine?"

"Sure," Trumaine said, "but . . ."

JoBob waved his hand behind his back and kept walking. When they got to the truck he opened the door on the driver's side for her. She hesitated, then got in with a jerky hopping motion. Her skirt was so tight she couldn't step up like a normal person.

"Okay," JoBob said. "Now start the motor and go home."

Her face crinkled up again. "You mean you . . . you're not coming? But I thought . . . I . . . ."

"No, I'm not coming! But *you're* going, and don't you ever come here again. Or to the barn either."

"Brat," she hissed. "You'll be sorry."

13
■■■

JoBob couldn't sleep. He tossed and turned
for hours while the wind rattled the tin on the roof
and whistled around the corner. Finally, he got up
and went outside to check the horses. Wind made
horses nervous and he was sure they'd all be spooking
and skittering in their stalls. The first one he checked
was Blue and he was lying down, with his legs tucked
underneath him and his head curled into his chest.
He didn't even stir when JoBob opened the door.
Sleep tight, JoBob told him silently, not wanting to
risk disturbing him by saying it out loud.

In the next stall Lulu was sleeping too. But he
was sure that Samantha, next to Lulu, would need
calming. She was unpredictable and jumpy, not placid
like Lulu. She was standing in the back corner of
her stall—her favorite place—and blinked sleepily
when JoBob opened her door. It always amazed him
that horses could sleep standing up.

He continued on down the aisle to find that all of

the horses were as quiet as the first three had been. One by one he shut the doors behind him, making sure they were latched. Didn't want one of them to get loose and go roaming over the showgrounds, where they could get a leg stuck in a garbage can or run through barbed wire and cut themselves up.

At the end of the aisle JoBob stretched and yawned. His body was tired and sleepy, but he knew there was no use going back to the tack room. He'd probably wake Trumaine up and his bedroll was so disheveled he couldn't possibly get comfortable. Besides, his mind was not sleepy. Not one bit. It was jumping and skittering the way he'd thought the horses were going to be. He sat down on a hay bale and drummed his feet—a muffled thud, not nearly as loud as the roaring of the wind. He wondered what time it was. Well, nighttime. Some time past midnight, probably, because he'd been tossing and turning for hours. Thick tufts of fog shut out the stars and crept up his pants, inside his shirt. He shivered. His mind shivered. He'd sounded tough talking to Darlene, but now, when he began to think about what was going to happen when he went home, he didn't feel tough at all. He felt small and frail and scared.

Maybe he could run away and join the circus. He thought about the colorful life they led, living in their own train, with the animals right along with them— the lions and tigers and gorillas in their own special cars painted yellow and red with bright stripes of blue and silver. Rolling into town, marching down the main street in the opening parade with the band playing, clowns capering, the tightrope walkers and tumblers and jugglers sashaying along while the barkers bellowed: "Come and see it, folks! Step right up. Come one, come all! Children of all ages, come see the Grrrreatest Show on Earth!" Seals balancing balls on their noses and pretty girls in spangles riding elephants, while boys not much older than he was whirled back and forth on unicycles, the silvery spokes of the wheels glittering in the sun. . . .

JoBob kicked the hay bale, no idle drumming this time, but a real hard kick. He didn't know how to juggle or ride a unicycle or swing on a trapeze. The circus was out. Well, he'd be a gypsy, then. Gypsies were horse traders and he knew something about that. They lived the same kind of colorful peripatetic life as the circus performers—traveling from place to place in wagons strung with pots and pans, bits of harness, tinkly bells, lanterns. He knew about them from a story Mrs. Gunderson read in second grade. He'd never forget it. How they cooked over an open fire, and did strange and fascinating things like looking into crystal balls and reading palms and tea leaves. The women wore purple and red and jade green laced with gold, and the men wore shiny boots and tight black pants, blousy shirts and gold chains. At night they played violins and everyone sang and danced, their teeth flashing in the flickering light from the fire while the trees bent over them and, nearby, water in the brook leaped and gurgled, silvery in the moonlight. Then, if there was any trouble, or if they just felt like it, they'd pack everything up and disappear down the road again, elusive as evening shadows. No one called them to account, or slapped them around. No sirree.

Only . . . only he'd never *seen* any gypsies. That idea was even sillier than the circus. If they existed at all, either they were dead, or they lived someplace like Yugoslavia or Hungary. Somewhere, at any rate, very far from any place he'd ever been. Not even in San Francisco had he seen anybody who looked like a gypsy. It was just a fantasy. Whereas the reality was back home where his father was probably already up, feeding the cocks a special mix for fight day, loading the cages into the truck with no one to help him. . . .

JoBob had been working with the cocks for years. He couldn't remember a time when he hadn't helped his father mix the feed, or taken a turn staying up at night with the incubating eggs to make sure the temperature stayed right. He helped massage them with alcohol and ammonia to make their skin tough, watched his father trim their feathers and fit the gaffs, and helped his father and Chet at home in the training sessions.

When JoBob was little, on fight days he used to hang around and watch the men, his eyes bugging out as they exchanged rolls of bills and passed hip flasks as they milled around before the fight started. Then they'd gather around the pit, not chatting any-more, their attention riveted on the action in the pit. They yelled, encouraging the bird they'd backed, and they sung out bets all the time, the money flying faster as the day progressed. JoBob hunched between them, his heart racing with excitement.

One of JoBob's jobs was to get rid of the dead cocks. He'd take the small body, still warm and dripping blood, and fling it onto the garbage pile. Sometimes his stomach lurched like he was going to throw up.

And once he watched the dead cock sailing through the air and when it landed JoBob looked at the heap of bright feathers resting among the orange peels and balled-up baling wire and burst into tears. Luckily, he was back behind the tractor shed and no one saw him. He went back to the pit like he was supposed to, and he saw the same familiar scene. The referee called "Pit!" and the birds were up and at each other, gaffs flashing, feathers flying, and the men were all crowded around, yelling and carrying on the way they always had. But it was like JoBob had been looking at it up until then without really *seeing* it. Now he saw the cocks being made to fight, and the men acting like it was exciting and important. Like, somehow, those birds made them important. But it wasn't true. It was cruel and mean and JoBob didn't want any part of it.

He didn't let on to his father right then, and he kept on going to the fights with him—because he had to. He even kept on getting rid of the dead ones too, trying not to think about what he was doing.

Somewhere in there he started riding. And going to horse shows, which meant that he had a good excuse to stay away from most fights. His father objected, of course. He grumbled, or got sarcastic, or just plain mean. But JoBob went to the show anyway. It was like Slim was some kind of Providence who saved him. In the last two years JoBob had been to only a few fights and even those were a few too many.

After Darlene had left that evening, JoBob hurried past the tack room where Slim and Irma were cleaning up. He needed to be alone so he could think. But he felt rather than saw Slim falling in behind him.

Then Slim called, "Slow down, JoBob, I want to talk to you."

JoBob didn't want to talk to anyone, not even Slim, but he supposed he'd have to sooner or later. After all, he'd be spending pretty much all the next day with him at the show and riding home with him in the cab of the van. He didn't know who he was maddest at—Darlene for coming and blabbing off at Slim and Irma, or his father for making her come. He didn't want anyone at the barn to know what kind of family he had.

He stopped and waited for Slim. Too late now. Good old Darlene had taken care of that.

"You sure you shouldn't have gone to help your daddy?" Slim asked.

"Yes, I'm sure. You didn't believe her, did you?"

"Well now." Slim started fiddling with his hat. "You sayin' she was talkin' fibs?"

"Oh . . ."

"Well now?"

"Sort of." JoBob dug his toe in the dirt and didn't look at Slim. "See, she can get real dramatic. She's planning on being a movie star and . . ."

"I'm talkin' about your daddy. She said he needed you."

"Oh, well . . . Anyway, you need me, right? And Blue. Blue needs me more than *he* does. We might be Reserve Champion. You know that, so how can you . . ."

"Shoot, this is just one horse show. There'll be others, you know."

JoBob bit his lip and cursed Darlene in his head. Now here was Slim sounding like he was taking her side. Slim was still talking: "Sure, I need you, but in an emergency I could make do. A person has obligations to his family."

"What if a person's family stinks?"

Slim raised his eyebrows. "They're still your family and everybody needs someone. It's damn hard to do everything all by yourself all the time."

"But that's what you do."

Slim made one of his noises, a sort of "hoo,hoo," whistling through his teeth. Then he took his hat all the way off and wiped his forehead with his handkerchief. Without his hat he looked different, and JoBob noticed all of a sudden how deep the lines were around his eyes and his mouth. "You don't know the half of it, and like I said . . ."

"What if your father wants you to do something wrong? Then what?" JoBob blurted.

Slim sighed and put his hat back on. "Well then, a person has a problem, don't he?"

Neither spoke for a minute. They just stood there, Slim fingering his hat, JoBob digging around in the dirt with his toe. Then Slim touched JoBob lightly on the shoulder. "Guess you just have to do what you think is right."

"That's what I *did.*"

"I reckon you did, son. I reckon you did."

Now JoBob wasn't so sure. The night around him seemed to be changing color, lightening almost imperceptibly. As the day began to dawn, cold and gray, the wind whipped fog through the stable rows. It

136

whisked away the gypsies and circus performers, and Slim's words too. What was real was his father's face when he was angry. The way the muscle in his jaw worked and his eyes glinted hard as gunmetal. JoBob's heart was colder than his feet. He'd never defied his father before. Not like that.

As JoBob did his morning chores, his mouth tasted like he hadn't brushed his teeth for a week, and his eyes were so gritty the air might as well have been sand. He wasn't working so well either. He gave Samantha Lulu's oats, which would send her right through the roof; she had plenty of get up and go without any help from oats. Then, when he went to get a doughnut and a cup of hot chocolate, he forgot to pay. The woman at the concessions stand yelled, "Hey, kid! You come back here, you rotten little punk!" JoBob slammed a quarter down on the counter and went back to the barn with "rotten little punk" ringing in his head.

While he was getting Samantha ready for Irma she stepped on his foot. "You stupid bitch!" he yelled and slapped her hard. That made her more nervous, so he had to spend an extra few minutes trying to calm her down while he tried to ignore the fact that his hand was smarting and that Slim would have said, "Tempers have got no place around horses." JoBob was falling apart, and on this day especially, he wanted to be sharp. And cool.

With his toes throbbing and swelling in his boot, he hobbled up to the ring with Samantha and when he got there discovered that he'd forgotten the rub rag and the number. When he went back to the barn to get them K.T. said, "You seen the wire cutters? I can't find them anywhere."

"In the toolbox," JoBob said. "Where they're supposed to be."

K.T. held up a bunch of neatly coiled baling wire that someone had stowed in the toolbox. "Maybe you threw them in the trash can?"

JoBob shrugged. *Had* he?

But then Slim was standing halfway between the ring and the barn yelling for him to hustle; it was almost time for Samantha to go in the ring.

Irma on Samantha had one of the best trips she'd ever had and wound up fifth. Irma came out of the ring with the pink ribbon, beaming. "How 'bout that? Wasn't she a good girl?" She patted Samantha and handed the reins to JoBob.

"Yeah," JoBob said.

"You can take her back to the barn now," Irma said in a flat voice, turning away.

JoBob's throat caught. It wasn't so often that Irma even got around. "I'm sorry," he said. "It was a real good round. Congratulations."

Irma turned back and smiled. "Thanks, JoBob." Then, "I know you're upset. Anything I can do to help?"

"No. But thanks anyway." He appreciated her concern. Slim's too. But what could they do? He'd made a decision. Now he'd have to face the consequences.

The rest of the day was pretty much like the morning. JoBob's body was wrapping Samantha for the trip home, taking down stall signs, stacking buckets, and unscrewing screw-eyes while his mind was already at home and his father was . . . Every time he came to that point he slammed on the brakes in his mind and refused to go any further.

The pandemonium of leaving day went on all around him—people dismantling tack rooms and packing trunks, loading trucks and vans—while the announcer's voice drifted down from the ring, calling the number of the horse in the ring, or the awards for the class just over, or urging the riders in the next class to come on up and start warming up.

By one-thirty the show grounds were already beginning to look deserted. Stall doors swung open on their hinges, bits of trash blew along the aisles, and kids poked through the empty stalls looking for pop bottles or other usable things that might have been left behind.

Then it was time to get Blue ready for his last two classes. JoBob got on and went up to the ring. He won the Bareback Eq and placed sixth in the Junior Working Hunter Stake. Not the best round he'd ever ridden, but not the worst either. K.T. got second, which meant that Charlie was Reserve Champion. He was real friendly as the three of them walked back to the barn, leading their horses with their right hands and holding their ribbons in their left. Trumaine and Lulu had placed tenth in the stake—their first ribbon of the show—and Trumaine was grinning from ear to ear.

"It was a good show," K.T. said.

"It sure was," Trumaine said. "You were a real good girl," he told Lulu enthusiastically, giving her a pat. Trumaine always said he did it for fun and didn't care whether he placed or not. So JoBob was surprised at Trumaine's enthusiasm and wished he could muster some of his own for Trumaine's sake. He hooked Blue's green sixth-place ribbon onto his bridle and held up his hand for Trumaine to slap.

Trumaine slapped it back. "It was a good show," JoBob said without really feeling it. It *had* been a good show, but his mind was running on what was going to happen a few hours from then when he got back home.

14

■■■

B<small>Y THE TIME</small> Slim's big green and white van left the showgrounds it was late afternoon. JoBob sank into the seat wishing that the drive home was a lot longer than an hour and a half. He needed time to think. He leaned his head back against the seat and the next thing he knew, Slim was shaking his knee.

"We're here."

His words flooded JoBob with panic. He'd gone to sleep when he should have been plotting a plan of action.

"We'll put the horses away now," Slim said. "Leave the rest of the stuff until tomorrow."

While they were unloading the horses JoBob wondered what his father had done about the fight. He still couldn't figure out why he'd wanted him to be there so bad. He hadn't been to a fight in a long time and there were lots of people hanging around at every fight with nothing much to do. Guys who would jump at the chance to help his father. He was

Gavin Draper, after all. Had some of the best cocks in all of California. So it had to be something else. *He needs someone he can trust,* Darlene had said. Someone who wouldn't talk when he did something cute, like slip some whiskey into the water of the cock that was going to be fighting his. Or something a whole lot cuter and more complicated than that. He and Chet had been working on some deal, JoBob was almost positive; but, because Chet had been in that accident, and because JoBob had stayed at the show, it had gotten messed up. JoBob started to shake. He should have gone with Darlene. He shouldn't have left his father like that.

It didn't take them long to unload the horses, and then JoBob took his stuff out of the van and put it in the back of Slim's truck. Way sooner than he wanted it to, Slim's truck was stopping on the road in front of his house. JoBob went around to the back to get his stuff. His hunt cap wouldn't fit in his suitcase, so he put it on his head, took the suitcase in one hand and the two silver trays Blue had won in the other. He watched the taillights disappear down the road, taking Providence along with them.

JoBob turned and walked slowly toward the house, threading his way through the piles of junk in the yard. His eyes weren't used to the dark and having both hands full made it harder to see somehow. He stumbled over something and almost lost his balance. Then Flea came streaking around from the back of the house, yelping with joy. JoBob set down his suitcase and the trays and knelt to pat her. "Good girl," he said. "Good girl. Did you miss me?" She jumped up

142

and licked his face. "I've got lots to tell you," JoBob said as Flea snuggled against him, her tail wagging. "But first I want you to tell me something." He paused and glanced at the house. He could see the light from the TV flickering in the living room, and around back the light from the kitchen spilled out onto the back porch. His father's truck was parked in the usual place, near the front porch, which destroyed one hope JoBob had had—that his father hadn't come home yet. "What's it like in there?" JoBob whispered to Flea. "Can you tell me?" All of a sudden Flea dropped down and froze as if she sensed danger nearby. JoBob felt it too. Then he realized what it was. His father. Standing on the front porch.

"Pop?"

"I don't see anybody else out here." His father's voice came through the dark. Noncommittal. "You going to come in or spend the night out there with that silly bitch?"

"Coming."

JoBob picked up his stuff and went around to the back with Flea padding along behind him. On the back porch she settled into her place with a sigh and JoBob stopped. *Run,* something told him. *Get out of here.* A flash of himself on the lam, all his possessions tied into a red bandanna dangling from a stick crooked over his shoulder, free as air, roaming over the wide surface of the earth . . . He looked at the sagging screen door, the weathered floorboards of the back porch. Face it. This is where he lived. He snuggled his fingers into Flea's ruff, gave her a last pat, and went inside.

His mother was at the sink washing dishes, and through the door to the front room he could see Darlene sitting in front of the TV putting polish on her fingernails. Seemed like she did her nails at least three times a day.

"Look what I won, Mom," JoBob said.

She dried her hands on the dish towel and took one of the trays. "Well, that's real pretty, JoBob." She turned it this way and that, then set it down on the kitchen table. "Did Blue win these? Or one of Slim's horses?"

"Blue," JoBob said, wondering if she knew how different it was. "And you should have heard what people said about him! Just about everybody there admired him. One guy, named Ted Huggles, he's a trainer at Blackstone Farm, this real fancy place in Santa Barbara, he said . . ."

All of a sudden JoBob heard himself, and he saw his mother with the polite smile, like she was trying to listen, trying to be pleased, and part of her really *did* care, really did want to know; but a whole lot bigger part of her, and him too, wasn't thinking about Blue or the show at all. Even when he was standing out on the front porch, where JoBob guessed his father still was, he could dominate the whole house. But maybe, just maybe, he was going to do one of his waiting acts. Let on like nothing had happened, then hit him with it when JoBob had nearly forgotten it. That was okay with JoBob. He was exhausted.

"I'm really tired," JoBob said. "I'll tell you about it tomorrow." He adjusted his hunt cap, the way he did right before he went into the ring. Then he picked up his suitcase and was halfway up the stairs to his

144

room when he heard the door bang on the front porch and the thu-thump, thu-thump of his father's step, the bad leg coming down more lightly than the good leg, as he crossed the front room.

JoBob stood on the steps, frozen.

Gavin advanced across the kitchen, the muscles in his jaw working, his eyes hard. Darlene appeared at the door to the front room, holding her left hand in a fan in front of her and blowing on her nails, while her eyes flicked between JoBob and their father.

"You come here, JoBob." His voice was flat and menacing.

JoBob came back down the stairs and set the suitcase down.

"Next time I send someone to get you, you come," his father said.

"I tried to get him to come," Darlene whined. "But he wouldn't. He just gave me a lot of lip."

"You stay out of this," Gavin said. "I already heard what you have to say." He turned back to JoBob. "Well?"

"I couldn't come. I had obligations. And . . . and we did real well. Look, I'll show you the ribbons." He knelt and started to open his suitcase.

His father's hand smacked down on his, hard, and his other grabbed his upper arm and jerked him to his feet. JoBob's hunt cap fell off his head and rolled across the floor, where it stopped near the door. He twisted and ducked, trying to get away, but his father's fingers dug into his arm and held him tight.

"You got obligations to *me!*" he said. "Know what you did?"

"No, sir."

"You queered one of the best deals I ever had goin'. *That's* what you did. You and that drugstore cowboy, Slim Abbott. I needed you to help get my cocks in the pit. But no. You've gotten too hoity-toity to help out your own father."

"You can have your old cocks," JoBob said. "They stink!" He hadn't meant to say that. Oh God, he hadn't, but the words blurted out. JoBob clapped his free hand over his mouth, scared now. *Really* scared.

"Stink?" Gavin yelled. "Old cocks! By God . . ."

"And I'm not going to do it ever again," JoBob heard himself blabber. "It's cruel! They shouldn't have to die!"

"So that's it," his father breathed, rolling his eyes up in disgust.

Then no one said anything. JoBob heard panting and gasping and he wasn't sure who it was. "My own son," Gavin went on, real quiet now, and ominous. "I swear to God."

This was more dangerous than yelling. He was like a snake coiled up and ready to strike. JoBob could feel the anger working beneath the coldness, but now that he'd said it, something was boiling up in him too—the anger and hurt that he'd kept to himself for so long he almost couldn't recognize it any longer. The way those dead cocks had felt in his hands, and the other things he'd seen and done, the sickness rising in him every time, and him stuffing it down, trying to keep on pretending that it didn't matter, that he didn't care. "They shouldn't have to die," he repeated.

"They don't feel it," his father said with a weird

146

little laugh. "They're just birds. Nothin' but a pea-sized brain will fit in a head that size. They don't even *know*. . . ." He paused and loosened his grip on JoBob's arm. Then let go.

Maybe it was over. Maybe JoBob had distracted him with this idea. It was only a second or two, but it felt like a very long time. JoBob edged backward toward the stairs, very slowly and warily. It didn't work. His father's hand grabbed his arm again.

"You turn into some lily-livered wimp? A hu-man-i-tarian like those nuts at the SPCA? You got balls, boy. That tenderhearted stuff is for those ladies down in town, all dressed up in hats and white gloves crooking their little fingers over teacups, jumping out of their pants at the *idea* of blood."

"Not me!" JoBob said. "You're the lily-livered wimp!"

His father stood stone still, like he'd thrown a bucket of cold water in his face, and his expression changed from anger to puzzlement. "How's that?"

"The war," JoBob said. "You were too scared to go fight in the war, so you have to make those cocks do what you couldn't."

A roar came out of him—loud and crazy as a stuck bull. In the same instant he pulled his belt off and was coming at JoBob, even though they were already so close it didn't seem possible. JoBob sidled backward, toward the door—the stairs—any escape, although he already knew it was too late to get away. Much too late . . .

Then time changed, and space. As if from a long way away, JoBob saw Darlene retreat into the front

147

room, heard his mother saying, "Gavin, don't," and his father yelling at her to shut up or she'd get it too. She stood for seconds? minutes? wringing her hands in the dish towel, then turned back to the sink and started rinsing the dishes in the dishpan. And his father, who had become two huge glittering eyes and two huge hands, which held him while the belt came down, moving almost lazily through the air; and landing then. And again. With a part of him JoBob felt it—with some other body that registered the pain—but then his mind went spinning off and took his body with it, pulling him down and down to a place where ordinary sound stopped and all he could hear was a strange kind of roaring. . . .

Then it was over. The greeny light from the TV was shining in the front room, his father was back in his body, his black hair falling loosely across his forehead, his hands threading the belt back through the loops, his face red and shiny with sweat, the dark hairs of his chest curling out of the plaid shirt open at the neck.

"Now you apologize," he said in a normal voice.

"I'm sorry," JoBob said.

His father heaved a deep sigh. "All right." Then he turned and went into the front room, sank into his chair in front of the TV.

JoBob picked up his suitcase and walked gingerly up the stairs to his room. He could feel his body again and it hurt all over. He wished he hadn't said he was sorry. He wasn't. He dropped his suitcase on the floor and fell across his bed. He turned his face

148

into the pillow and pounded the mattress. He wished his father was dead, like K.T.'s father. Then he could wear his RAF cap and, when anybody came over, show them the picture of him with his squadron and speak about him, not in hushed tones exactly, but in a different tone, as if he were not quite ordinary. As if the dying, the having been in the war, moved him over to some other plane and kept him there forever and ever and ever.

JoBob pounded at the mattress again. His father dead wouldn't be any such good as K.T.'s dad, because his father really was a lily-livered wimp. Oh sure, he had the 4-F. He had the bad leg, but they would have taken him in the army if he'd tried. Or the RAF. They'd take almost anybody during the Battle of Britain when the whole of England had come close to being blown out of the water by hordes of Messerschmitts that kept on coming and coming. But he hadn't tried. He got off on the 4-F and then he got a job over in Oakland at the bomber assembly plant, because he was a skilled mechanic, and he said that was of equal importance to the national defense. *More* important. Because a pilot without a plane was no use to anybody, and few could put an engine together the way Gavin could. But he hadn't even done that for very long. He never did *anything* for very long. Except mess around with those cocks and sit around at Riley's Tavern.

JoBob wished he could get back at him. Beat *him* up. Punch and punch until he said "uncle"; but he wasn't nearly strong enough. . . .

He jerked out of his half-sleep with a startle, cold

and sore, lying on top of the covers in his clothes with the light on. He sensed someone in the room. Opened one eye and turned his head. His mother. She stood in the doorway with a bowl in her hands. "I brought you some soup," she said. "Thought you might be hungry."

"I'm not," JoBob said, and turned toward the wall.

She stood there for a long time. Then he heard her footsteps creak across the floor and the bowl being set on the table beside his bed. Her hand reached out, smoothed his forehead. "Joby, honey, he didn't mean it. He was just real upset. Chet being in the accident and all . . ."

"He didn't *mean* it?"

"Oh, well . . . He's your father. He was counting on you."

"Slim was counting on me, too. And Slim wasn't doing anything illegal."

"Illegal?"

"Yes! It's all illegal, don't you know that?"

"Oh, honey, I don't know. That's men's stuff. I just let him . . ."

JoBob sighed. She always did take Gavin's side. No reason why she would change now. "Well, it's all water under the bridge now, right? We ought to let bygones be bygones." Two of her favorite expressions.

She brightened considerably. "That's right. And forgive. Those trays sure are pretty. Don't know what I'll do with them, but . . . Now you take some of this soup. It's hot and it's nourishing. Alphabet-vegetable, your favorite."

150

"Sure, Mom." It *had* been his favorite when he was a little kid. He and Darlene used to pick out the letters and try to make words. But that was when he was six or seven years old, which was the last time he could recall that he'd said it was his favorite. That's the way his mother was, though. Treated him half the time like he was still in elementary school. He wondered if she knew that he was fifteen now— inside, as well as outside. That he was way past being a little kid in the things that he thought and felt. The things that he *knew*. Then he decided that he didn't want her to know. It would shock the hell out of her.

She smoothed her skirt and started toward the door. "Well, I'm going to bed now. Tomorrow's Monday, you know. You set your alarm? Horse shows are nice, but school is important."

JoBob didn't answer and she came close again. "Never mind the alarm. I'll wake you up. And I'll make you some cornmeal mush. That'll start the day right."

She went back across the room and when she got to the door she stopped. He could tell from the way she looked that she was going to do one of her Bible things.

Sure enough. "You know what Luke says: 'Judge not, and ye shall not be judged: condemn not, and ye shall not be condemned: forgive, and ye shall be forgiven.'"

JoBob knew there was no sense in arguing, so he just said, "Sure." She gave him one of her sad smiles and shut the door. He sat on the edge of his bed

151

and tried a sip of soup. It was still hot and it felt good in his stomach. It had been a long day and he *was* hungry.

His mother confused him so much. Why should he forgive his father when *he* hadn't done anything near as wrong as his father had? But his mother, as always with his father, got real selective. She wasn't telling his father that he ought not to judge JoBob, that he ought to forgive him; JoBob was sure of that.

He finished his soup and put on his pajamas. Then he switched out the light and crawled under the covers. He was bone tired and ached all over. Then he remembered Mariko. How he'd thought about going to her house when he got home on Sunday—Sunday, today— how he was going to tell her about the show and ask her to go mushrooming. How his biggest worry was whether or not he would have the nerve to do it. He wanted to laugh. Or maybe puke. His father had a real talent for messing up his plans. Tonight was bad enough. Worse, he doubted that he'd heard the end of it.

He was drifting off to sleep when he had an idea that jerked him wide awake. Next time his father had a fight out there JoBob would call the law. He'd go to town to a pay phone and talk into the telephone through a handkerchief and he'd tell them where the fight was. He'd give them his father's name and directions out to their place and then they'd come in the Black Marias with the red lights twirling on top. They'd pile out of the cop cars with their guns and billy clubs hanging down the sides of their legs, where they could get them in a minute if they got any guff from his father or Chet or any of the others. And they'd haul 'em off to jail and lock 'em up and that would fix his wagon, all right. His father wouldn't lift a hand against him, ever again, or make him do anything with those damned cocks either.

15
■■■

NEXT MORNING JoBob's mother woke him up and, sure enough, she had cooked cornmeal mush, which had been one of his favorites when he was a little kid, and still was. When JoBob and Darlene and their mother left, Gavin was still in bed, which was par for the course. The only thing that could get him out of bed before nine or ten o'clock was a cockfight.

JoBob was looking forward to seeing Mariko at the bus stop. He wasn't positive he was going to say anything to her—she did have a sort of standoffish manner when other people were around. But who knew? Lots of things were changing. Maybe he would say something; and maybe she wouldn't be standoffish. She hadn't been that evening before the show and he hadn't seen her since. JoBob stood at the bus stop out on the highway looking back toward her house, thinking that any minute he'd see her coming down the road. She was just a tad late. Although, with another part of him, he knew already that she wasn't coming. She was never late. When the bus came, he got on and sat down in his and Trumaine's usual seat, feeling grumpy.

When Trumaine got on, JoBob only half-listened because he was wondering what had happened to Mariko. Was she sick? Or what? Probably sick, he decided. There'd been a lot of flu going around that year. Then he had an idea: after school he'd go over to her house and take her the homework assignments. That would be a good excuse. He didn't give two figs about homework. His mother was always after him to make good grades, but he didn't see the point; so he did just enough work to pass from one grade to the next. A C was as good for that as an A, and it was a lot less work. He knew that Mariko cared, though. She'd always been near the top of the class.

After school he went to the barn. Monday was Slim's day off and the barn was closed. It was rest day for the horses too. But Mondays after a show were different. No riding to do, but a lot of other work—unpacking the van and putting everything back where it belonged.

When he got home he dumped his book satchel on the back porch, said hello to Flea, and told her to stay put. Then he marched resolutely down the road toward the Kawabatas' house. Halfway there he stopped, all the resolution draining out of him. If she was sick, then she'd be in bed, so he wouldn't be able to talk to her. He'd have to talk to her mother instead. Or maybe her grandmother—but that would be impossible: she didn't speak English. Well, he'd

155

call Mariko on the phone, then. He turned around to go home to call her and he was part-way there when he stopped again. If he called her on the phone Mabel Tompkins, who listened to every conversation anyone had on the party line, would hear it, and probably Edna Nixon, the operator, too. The mere thought of them listening made him blush, so he just stood there in the middle of the road having no idea about what to do next.

Well, maybe he'd go over there tomorrow. No, he said to himself, tomorrow's not going to be any different. Maybe she was just a little bit sick—a cold or something. Not sick enough to be in bed, but just sick enough so she couldn't go to school. Right! That's the way it was going to be. He turned around again and marched back down the road, turned up the Kawabatas' front walk, and was about to knock on the front door when his courage failed him again. No one at his house ever used the front door, so probably no one at their house did either. If he did that, they'd think he was a really stupid person. He ought to go around to the back. He was standing on the front doorstep with his face hanging out, thinking that he almost certainly ought to go around to the back, when he noticed a movement in one of the windows of the front room. He'd been seen, so that settled it. He knocked.

The door opened right away and his heart sank. Her grandmother.

"Good afternoon," JoBob said, polite as he could, thinking that maybe she would understand something as simple as that. He had to say something.

156

She nodded her head in a kind of half bow.

"Uh, is Mariko at home?"

She opened the door wide and stepped backward with another bowing gesture, so JoBob felt that she was asking him to come in.

He stepped inside. She stepped backward another couple of steps, then, still facing him, turned her head and said something in Japanese.

Mariko's mother appeared from the kitchen and JoBob had to go through the whole rigamarole again—asking if Mariko was home, saying good afternoon, being as polite as he could, feeling more and more uncomfortable.

"Yes, she is. Would you like to sit down?"

The two women disappeared through the door to the kitchen and JoBob sat on the couch. On the edge of the couch. He could hear them in the kitchen talking in Japanese and that was weird as hell. What were they saying? Then he heard some English too. Mariko. Good, at least she wasn't in bed.

After a few minutes he started to look around. The floors were bare—smooth polished wood with no rugs. Not a whole lot of furniture, either—a couch, which he was sitting on, with a coffee table in front of it. Across the room two armchairs with a narrow table in between. On the table a dark red vase with an arrangement of irises in it, their purple splash the brightest color in the room. It was all extremely clean and neat. His father was always calling them "dirty Japs," which showed how much he knew. Not even Trumaine's house was this clean and his mother had a maid.

JoBob started to fidget. He'd been sitting there an awfully long time. Had they forgotten he was there? Good—he could get up and walk out the front door, forget the whole thing. They were still talking in the kitchen and he picked out Mariko's voice again.

"Mama, please, it's all *right.*"

More Japanese, then Mariko again, "But the doctor said I shouldn't walk." Then her mother said something, in English, JoBob was pretty sure, but so low he couldn't catch the words. Then Mariko said, "All right," again. Then thumps and noises that sounded like furniture being moved. Mariko appeared at the door on crutches with her mother behind her holding a footstool.

"Hey, what happened to you?" JoBob asked.

"Sprained my ankle. It was silly—I was just stepping off the front porch, but I stepped wrong and my ankle just caved in."

"That's too bad," JoBob said. "Uh, I was going to ask if you wanted to go looking for mushrooms, but . . ." Now why did he go and say that when he'd already decided not to? Since she couldn't go roaming around in the woods with a sprained ankle, it sounded silly.

She smiled, then hobbled over to one of the armchairs and sat down. Her mother set the footstool in front of her and Mariko put her foot up on it. "I'm supposed to keep my foot up so the swelling will go down."

Her grandmother sat in the other armchair and her mother went back to the kitchen.

"Sorry to keep you waiting so long. I told Mama

158

you could come into the kitchen, because I'm not supposed to move much. But she said it wasn't proper, so . . ." She smiled and shrugged.

Her mother came in with a tray, which she set on the coffee table in front of the couch where JoBob was sitting. She knelt beside the table, took a teapot from the tray, and poured into a little blue and white china cup with no handles. She handed it to Mariko's grandmother. Then she poured another and gave it to JoBob. Then she poured one for Mariko and, finally, one for herself. No one said a word during all this and JoBob thought how dumb it was for him to have come. It was worse than being in church. Only it wasn't church. It was a tea party of sorts. What his mother would call a social occasion. But social occasions required conversation and no one that he noticed was doing much talking. So it was up to him. And he was lousy at this. Especially with Mariko sitting right across the room from him looking somewhat like the Mariko he'd talked to in the woods last Tuesday, but more like the one he'd known way before that—formal and distant. Her grandmother was looking at him too, her eyes so dark they were almost black; her mother was looking down, but JoBob knew that she knew that he was there and he was expected to do something. They were all expecting him to do something. What?

Then he remembered a story he'd read about a Navajo boy. The boy had a problem and went to consult one of the elders. He stood outside the hogan and asked permission to come in. Permission was given and he went in. The elder was sitting on a rug and didn't look up or speak when he went in. The boy, who was impetuous and very worried about his problem, opened his mouth to blurt it out. But something made him shut it again, and he sat down. The elder lit a pipe and inhaled. Exhaled. He handed the pipe to the boy and he inhaled. Exhaled. Handed the pipe back. They exchanged the pipe a few more times and then the elder set it aside. The atmosphere had changed. The boy was no longer nervous.

"You are learning the ways," the elder said. "When you bring so much outside matter into the hogan I cannot hear your spirit."

Even then the boy didn't talk. He bowed his head and waited for the elder.

"I am ready to hear you now," he said.

JoBob sipped his tea trying to imagine that it was a pipe, that it was their ritual, and he was doing it right.

Still no one spoke. Mariko adjusted her foot on the stool. Her grandmother sipped her tea. Out of the corner of his eye JoBob could see Mariko's mother, sitting on the couch to his left, also sipping her tea. JoBob waited. Nothing happened. Finally, he decided they might be able to sit like that for hours, but he couldn't. He wanted to get out of there.

"I . . . uh . . . I'm sorry about your ankle. I thought you might be sick so I brought the homework assignments."

"Thank you. I'll be able to come to school in another day or so, but I don't want to get behind. Thank you very much."

"You're welcome."

160

Another silence. Then Mariko said, "Where were you last week? I thought you might be sick."

"No. I was at a horse show over in Sacramento." Here was his chance to tell her about the show, but he couldn't do it with her grandmother and her mother sitting there.

"Oh. I didn't know you went to horse shows."

"Yeah. I mean yes." His mother was always telling him not to say "yeah." JoBob sipped his tea, which was pale green and didn't taste like anything much.

"Well, I've got to go now," he said, setting his cup down on the tray. Then he got up, and Mariko's grandmother and mother stood up too.

"Thank you for the tea," he said.

"JoBob?"

"What?"

"Where's the homework assignment?"

"The homework?" He patted his pockets, feeling really stupid because he'd left it at home in his book satchel. "I, uh, I *thought* I put in my pocket, but I guess I left it in my book satchel. You want it?"

"Yes, I do. I thought that's why you came."

"No, not really. I mean, yeah. I mean—" Oh Lord, everything coming out of his mouth was wrong, but how could a body think with those three women staring at him? "I'll run home and get it, okay?"

He didn't wait for her to say okay and he didn't say good-bye or anything to her mother, either. He was too embarrassed. He ran down the road, grabbed his satchel off the back porch, and ran back. He knocked on the door again, handed the assignment to her mother, and left, running again. He wished he could run right out of his body; or, better yet, backward through time, back through the whole scene, canceling it out.

Well, going to her house was strange and unusual, all right. Wouldn't catch him doing that again.

Flea came barging out to meet him and JoBob said, "Okay, okay. I'm happy to see you too. And I'm not going off anywhere else this afternoon. I'm home now." He dumped his book satchel on the back porch again and went out to do his chores.

He meant what he'd decided last night. He was never going to another fight, and he wasn't going to play like the referee or any of that kind of stuff, either. But he'd been feeding and watering the cocks and cleaning the runs since he was a little kid and, as long as he was still living there, he figured he'd better keep on doing it. It wouldn't be for much longer, anyway. When the opportunity arose he *was* calling the cops.

Flea flopped down in her usual place at the beginning of the runs by the feed shed. She knew the routine. While JoBob was doing his chores, she'd lie there with one eye on him, and then, when he was done, she'd jump up and go get a stick or a ball and they'd play fetch.

JoBob mixed up the feed then went down the line, filling the feed troughs and cleaning out the water bowls, then refilling them with fresh water from the big watering can he carried with him. He used to do them one at a time—carrying each bowl down to the spigot, rinsing it, refilling it, carrying it back.

162

Then he'd thought of the watering can, which was a lot more efficient. He only had to make three trips down to the spigot instead of twenty or thirty. He was going along doing all this without thinking about it. Wasn't the sort of thing that needed thinking about. Then he came to the pen in the middle of the second side and he noticed it was empty. Something went twang in the back of his brain. This was the one where Emerald had been. Or the Emerald look-alike. One of them, at any rate.

He went back to the beginning of the row where Emerald had always been before his father switched him. In it was a young black cock who used to be farther down the row on the same side. JoBob hadn't even noticed when he'd fed and watered him.

He started back down the path, stopping to look into each pen. No Emerald. No Emerald Jr., either. "What do you think of that, Flea?"

Flea got up and wagged her tail, her head cocked quizzically.

"I think I'm beginning to get it," JoBob said slowly. " 'Member how Chet said 'it just proves our point' when I got them mixed up?"

Flea cocked her head to the other side.

"They were going to switch them at the fight. Put Emerald Jr. in the big one against the Peruvian bird and put Emerald in the novice fight against some cock who wouldn't have a chance against Emerald; and bet on the Peruvian bird in the big fight and Emerald in the other one. Two slam dunks, right?"

This time Flea gave a little yelp, as if she were beginning to understand it too.

JoBob whistled. His father was a pretty high roller, even when the odds weren't so great. And with a surefire deal like that, he must have really shot his wad. "Only he'd have to switch them at the very last minute, because they'd get caught in the prefight inspection. So because I wasn't there, and because Chet wasn't there . . ." It was one of his better scams, but the executing of it would have been tricky and something clearly had gone wrong, which was why his father had been so angry.

JoBob whistled again. Considering all this, he'd gotten off pretty lightly last night. His father *hated* to lose. JoBob was a little scared too. The fight crowd was a pretty tough bunch and they wouldn't appreciate Gavin pulling a fast one like that—or trying to. And what if he'd bet something he didn't have? Something he couldn't afford to lose? Face it, there were six ways to Sunday his father could be in pretty deep trouble.

16

■■■

A FEW DAYS later JoBob came home and found his mother standing at the kitchen sink with some of the trophies he'd won stacked on the drain board. She was polishing a silver bowl he'd won with Sophie at the Napa show in March. When he came in, she turned off the water and wiped her hands on a dish towel. Turning toward him, she said, "I ran into Mrs. Watson down in town today. She said you're a real good rider."

JoBob was amazed, not so much that his mother was quoting Trumaine's mother—she'd always been impressed with the Watsons—but the way she was looking at *him*, as if something about him were new and different.

He shrugged. "Blue's a good horse. He does most of it."

"Well now," she said, "way I heard it, Trumaine has a nice horse too, and expensive, and he doesn't win nearly the things you do. That right?"

165

"Yeah. But Trumaine thinks it's just fun."

"And you?"

He shrugged again, trying to hide the uneasiness he felt by appearing unconcerned. "I think it's fun, too," he said. Her being so interested had him scared. Like she was the sun and he was a cool shy moss growing deep in the woods that could be withered up by too much brightness.

His mother loved success. She liked to talk about her great-uncle, Tobias Whitfield, who was General Jackson's cousin; and Stonewall Jackson, everybody knew, was Lee's right arm. If he hadn't been killed at Chancellorsville by one of his own men shooting loony in the dark, why the Confederacy would have won the war and . . . She could go on and on about the glorious victories at Manassas and Harpers Ferry and Fredericksburg—before Jackson was killed of course—like it had happened five years ago, instead of a hundred. Like it made some kind of difference. Tobias Whitfield was just a cousin of Jackson's by marriage, but to hear her talk, the great Stonewall Jackson might as well have been her own father.

She dried off the bowl and set it down on the kitchen table beside a bunch of sweet peas. The bowl caught slivers of light from the sun, which was slanting through the windows and cast them back out into the room in a myriad of sparkles.

"Don't these look nice?" Almost as if she were talking to herself.

The pale pinks and lavenders of the flowers lent new color to the kitchen and, as she arranged them in the bowl, they quivered delicately, filling the room with their sweetness, and making the whole room feel different. Then JoBob noticed that the room *was* different. The windows were sparkling clean and the floor was newly mopped.

"What's going on?" he asked.

"Hm?" She looked up absently, as if she'd forgotten he was there.

"The floor. The windows." Before she had time to answer, JoBob went into the front room, pretty sure what he would find when he got there. Sure enough, the coffee table was dusted. A candy dish he'd won last year was filled with mints and sitting on the end table, which was also dusted. And a new flowered cover was spread over the couch, so if you didn't know the green plush underneath had lost its pile and was worn so thin in places the kapok was threatening to erupt, you'd think it was a perfectly respectable couch. One like they had at Trumaine's house.

JoBob went to the doorway into the kitchen and stood with one hand on the doorjamb looking at his mother. "What's the deal? How come you put a new cover on the couch?"

"Oh well," her hand fluttered toward her throat, "that old one was worn right through and Woolworth's had a sale on chintz, ten cents a yard. Looks nice, don't you think? And Flora . . ."

"Who's Flora?"

"Hm?" the flutter of her hand again. "Flora *Watson*, of course. I invited her to tea. Thought she might like to see your trophies. . . ."

"She's coming *here?* Today?" His mother had known

167

Trumaine's for years and they'd never called each other anything except "Mrs. Draper" and "Mrs. Watson." JoBob never even knew her name was Flora.

"Well, yes, honey. No . . . no . . . tomorrow. I'll call in sick, make some little tea sandwiches like my grandmother used to make back in Virginia when I was a girl. Cucumber and watercress. You think you could go down to the river and pick me some watercress? They'll look real nice on that tray you won, and maybe I'll cut some radishes, like little flowers, give a spot of color, don't you see? And . . ."

"Shit!"

"You watch it, JoBob. You're not too old to have your mouth washed out with soap."

JoBob sank into a chair and dropped his head into his hands. Next thing she'd probably start in on Tobias Whitfield. But she went on, in a new coy voice. "She just happened to mention, you know, to me in town today . . . She said, 'Cerise, I'd just love to see some of JoBob's trophies. Trumaine said JoBob won two classes at the Sacramento show—real nice silver ones. And Trumaine, well, he brings home all these different colored *ribbons,* and not so many of those, either, but the only trophy he ever got is this old gilt horse planted on a kind of wood base—from a schooling show two winters ago. . . .' So what could I do? I said it would be a pleasure. Maybe she'd like to drop by for tea, so . . ."

JoBob couldn't stand it any longer. He got up and headed for the door.

"Where are you going?"

"Feed the chickens," he said over his shoulder, and

the door was thwacking behind him before she could say anything else. She could hardly tell him not to go. They were his chores, after all.

Flea came running up as soon as he stepped onto the back porch. Then she stopped her headlong rush toward him and yelped a questioning bark—she knew something was wrong. JoBob muttered some of the things he'd been on the verge of saying to his mother— a good long lick of cuss words. That made him feel better and he set off for the chicken runs, explaining the rest of it to Flea as they went. Mrs. Watson had been out there a few times before—when he and Trumaine were too young to ride the bus or their bicycles— but she'd never been inside the house that JoBob knew of. "She's gone right off her gourd," he told Flea. "You can't cover up the plaster falling off the ceiling with Woolworth's cloth, or the missing boards on the front porch. What does she want to do this to me for?"

Flea looked at him with her wise eyes and her tail waved tentatively, wanting to wag, but not yet sure enough to. JoBob stroked her head. "Up until now she hardly paid any attention to what I won, but just let Flora Watson say one word and—well, I tell you, honey, it's a whole different ball game. If she thinks it's so great, why didn't she tell me at the time?"

He wished Flea could talk. She could probably give him an explanation that made sense. The whole time he was tending to the chickens, he was trying to figure it out. And when he finally got it, he laughed. It was so simple, how could he have been so dim? She

169

wanted to show off. She wanted to one-up Mrs. Watson with his trophies.

When he was finished with the cocks he headed for the woods. It was still full light and he hadn't exactly seen any signs of supper being cooked. He wasn't ready to go back in the house yet. While he walked he thought about taking all the trophies and burying them out in the woods. Then his mother would be in a real pickle when Mrs. Watson came to tea. Then, by slow degrees, he began to feel different. He remembered the way she'd looked at him over the sweet peas in the bowl, her eyes glowing with pride, and he began to feel proud too. He'd finally done something that pleased her.

He'd been thinking about turning professional when he was eighteen, being a trainer. Riding was the one thing he was really good at and you could make pretty good money at it, too, so what better thing for a man to do? Up until now he'd said something once or twice about being a trainer and his mother said that was low class. Then the next minute she'd start talking about how the show people were high and mighty and he shouldn't go getting uppity notions. Not that he cared what she said, really; it was his life. He stopped and broke off a branch, snapped off the leaves and twigs. Flea jumped up in the air and barked with excitement at the sight of the branch. JoBob flung it down the path ahead of them and she bounded after it; then brought it back, holding it firmly in her jaws and growling playfully. She crouched down onto her front paws and JoBob wrestled the stick from her. Then he raised his arm to throw it again and she was running before he'd released it. While she was bringing the stick back JoBob realized that he *did* care what his mother thought. It was real nice to have her be proud of him, like that.

He sat at the supper table listening to his father raving about the money his mother had spent at Woolworth's and he tried to get his mind to detach, but he couldn't do it.

Usually all his father had to do was raise his voice, or threaten, and his mother would simmer down. But this time she kept going on about how it was her money, she earned it after all, and she was tired of living in such a dump. Next paycheck she got, she was ordering a new carpet for the front room from the Sears' catalogue and maybe some new curtains too. She'd noticed a sale on paint at Watson's Hardware, so maybe JoBob could take a Saturday or a Sunday and put a new coat of paint on the front room—it sure was nice somebody around here had some pride. . . .

JoBob nearly choked on his iced tea when she said that, because he figured that was all the excuse his father needed to light into him, but Gavin laughed and said, "You do that, honey. Then maybe you can have the Ladies' Aid Society out here too."

His mother made a noise close to a giggle and said, "Maybe I will. As I was saying, when I met Flora down in town today, she allowed as how . . ."

JoBob knew what was coming next and he tried to figure a way out, but nothing came to him. If he tried to leave, it would only call attention to him;

then he'd get it for sure. The trouble was, the attention already was on him. His mother was rattling on about what a good rider he was, and what a valuable horse Blue was—at least that's what *Flora* said at any rate. . . . JoBob sat there and prayed that she'd stop. Seemed like she was *trying* to rile his father.

"That so?" Gavin said mildly when she paused for breath. "Maybe this horse nonsense is good for something, after all." He gave JoBob a strange speculative look, which was worse than any yelling he'd ever done. Much worse. Raised the hairs on the back of JoBob's neck and turned his insides quivery.

But his mother took his comment for approval and started off again, this time about some material she'd seen in Woolworth's that would make a real pretty graduation dress for Darlene.

His father agreed that it sounded nice, but maybe she ought to get something with some real class to it. Some real Irish lace, maybe. After all, they only had one daughter and she'd only graduate from high school once. That made JoBob nearly choke again. Only one thing you could say for sure about his father and that was: you never knew what he was going to do next. But by then they were off onto Darlene's dress and they'd stopped paying attention to him. So he excused himself, saying that he had homework to do, and went up to his room.

Up in his room he set his book satchel down. He took out the books and set them on the floor: *History of the Ancient World, Algebra I, English Composition.* He opened his notebook and looked at the assignments. There was hardly a month left of school, and he was

172

glad of that. For nearly the first time in his life, he envied Darlene. Graduating. Never having to go to school again. In three more years JoBob would be graduating too, and it wouldn't be a minute too soon. Trumaine said he was thinking about going to college, but JoBob thought he was crazy. He wasn't going to school one day more than he had to. Well, he'd be out of the ninth grade in a few weeks and he figured he'd done enough work for this year. He set his notebook on top of *English Composition* and took out *Training Hunters, Jumpers and Hacks,* by General Harry D. Chamberlin. General Chamberlin had won a gold medal in the Olympics. He'd established the Army Horse Show Team at Fort Riley, and had been the commander of the Second Cavalry Regiment there, too. Slim had been in that regiment. JoBob ran his fingers over the cover of the book before he opened it, feeling the same thrill he always did: a book written by someone who knew someone he knew. A book about something important and useful, never mind all those equations, and kings and queens who'd been dead a lot longer than a body wanted to think about.

He turned to chapter two, "Details of Conformation," and looked at the diagrams of galloping types, jumping types, trotting types, comparing, as he'd done in the past, Blue with the diagrams. The angles of Blue's ilium and ischium were great. So were his scapula and humerus. JoBob read on, about all the different joints, smiling at "Beauties," because every time old General Chamberlin could have been describing Blue. JoBob smiled at "Faults," too, because Blue didn't have any of those.

173

Downstairs he could hear his mother and father, still going at it. His mother's voice rattling along a mile a minute, his father's an occasional thrum, thrum, like the bass in a band. Didn't sound like they were arguing, but you never knew when that would change. JoBob looked back at the book, but the print was going squiggly and his mind felt fuzzy. The book sagged down on his chest and he fell asleep.

17

. . .

NEXT MORNING his head was even fuzzier. He got out of bed and the room tilted at strange angles. His knees felt like water and he fell back into bed. When his mother called up the stairs that he was going to be late if he didn't shake a leg, he said that he didn't feel so good. She came up and took his temperature and said he certainly was sick—seemed like everybody was coming down with the flu—matter of fact, she was scheduled to work overtime today because Shirley and Dorette had been out sick yesterday and Bonnie Prather had worked overtime. But she *had* invited Flora Watson to tea and she certainly wasn't going to cancel that. Matter of fact, it was a sort of a godsend really—with so many people coming down with the flu no one was going to doubt that she was sick too. Of course she had at least two weeks of sick leave saved up and if she said she was sick, then she was; but try telling Mrs. Henderson, the supervisor, that when she was in one of her moods.

She brought JoBob some aspirin and a cool cloth for his forehead and a cup of hot water with lemon juice and sugar in it. Whenever anybody was sick she always brought the cup of hot water with lemon and sugar. Said her grandmother had made it for her when she was a girl and it was better than most medicine you had to pay an arm and a leg for at Selkirk's Pharmacy. Then she started going on about the tea again. Said she was going to the river to get some watercress since JoBob had forgotten to do it the evening before, but she'd be back in an hour or so and he'd be all right until then, wouldn't he?

A little while later JoBob heard the back door bang shut and Darlene singing as she headed down the road to the bus stop. The back door banged again, which he figured would be his mother going down to the river. A while after that he heard his father messing around in the kitchen and then he left too. Then it was really quiet. He could hear the hum of the Frigidaire in the kitchen and Flea getting up and resettling herself on the back porch.

For a few days JoBob was so sick he didn't notice much except his mother coming to take his temperature or bring him something to drink. Then his fever started to go down and the days stopped fuzzing into each other. What a time to be sick. School would be out in three weeks and then they were going to go up to Yreka to the Siskiyou County Fair. That was JoBob's favorite horse show. Besides the horse show, there was the fair—4-H kids with their heifers and lambs and rabbits; ladies with jars of jam and quilts and cakes; and all kinds of other exhibits. There was the midway with the Ferris wheel whirling, girls shrieking on the rides, the calls of the barkers standing outside the sideshow tents pattering at the people passing by, trying to lure them inside. Smells of cotton candy and peanuts and hot dogs. And all the different booths—roulette and ringtoss and the baseball throw— with the shelves behind each booth lined with gaudy prizes. He and Trumaine always had a ball at the midway.

There was a racetrack too. When the horn sounded and the horses headed out of the paddock, their long Thoroughbred legs trotting easily while the Appaloosa and grade ponies cantered at their sides, the jockeys' silks brilliant dots of color amid the grays and browns of the horses, JoBob got a surge of excitement like nothing else he'd ever felt. He'd sit on the edge of his seat, then stand up when they swept around the clubhouse turn, his voice roaring along with the rest of the crowd. Slim called it the Leaky Roof Circuit. Said those horses weren't real quality like you had down in San Francisco at Bay Meadows or in Los Angeles at Hollywood Park. "Still," he said, "somethin' about seein' a horse run gets my blood to goin'." It got JoBob's too.

Right before JoBob got sick they'd been talking about that show at the barn. "It *is* the Leaky Roof Circuit," Slim said, "but it's a hell of a lot of fun, and it'll be a nice kind of warm-up for you all—for them A shows down south, which will be coming up pretty quick." So it was a terrible time for JoBob to be sick. He needed to get Blue tuned up for the show and Sophie, too. He and Blue had made a good start at the Sacramento show and JoBob had a feeling that it was the beginning of a roll. But him lying around in bed wasn't much help to Blue.

After a week JoBob started to get restless, even though he was still sick. His mother said he might as well face it, the ten-day flu was the ten-day flu. She was right. On the tenth day JoBob felt almost normal and on the eleventh, which happened to be a Saturday, he woke up feeling great. He ate breakfast and was heading for the barn while the dew was still on the grass. It felt wonderful to be well again, to be outside again, to have two whole days he could spend at the barn before he had to go back to school. He couldn't wait to see Blue. He hadn't seen him for ten whole days, which was the longest time ever. He thought about his white face sticking over his stall door and the way he whinnied at JoBob when he came in. Now that he was about to see him again, JoBob realized how much he'd missed him and he walked faster.

JoBob went into the barn and took a doughnut out of the box on Slim's desk. Saturdays, instead of cookies, Irma brought doughnuts.

"Hey, Blue," JoBob called as he walked down the aisle.

"Hey, Blue," he called again when he didn't appear. "Blue-oo!" raising his voice on the last syllable, almost like a yodel. His special call. When Blue still didn't appear, JoBob decided that he must be asleep. That was strange, though, because Gustavo fed in the morning as soon as it was light and no horse that JoBob had ever seen would sleep when he had a fragrant pile of alfalfa in front of him. He quickened his step.

178

Maybe something was wrong. Maybe Blue was sick or he'd gotten cast in his stall—his legs pinioned against the walls, his body scrunched up in a sandwich, his eyes rolling helplessly, waiting for someone to come and help. Why hadn't Gustavo noticed? Why hadn't Slim? Horse could hurt himself bad when he got cast. JoBob practically ran the last few yards to his stall, then stopped before he opened the door to collect himself. If Blue *was* cast, he didn't want to panic him further by opening the door too suddenly. Horses hated being trapped. Went back to the days when they were wild, Slim said. A wild horse's main defense was flight, and if he was trapped, then he was easy pickin's for any mountain lion or wolf that came along, so they'd thrash and flail, do anything to get loose. Sometimes they fought so hard they'd rupture a tendon, or have a heart attack. Or . . .

"Oh God," JoBob said, "please be all right, Blue." Then he opened the door, prepared for anything. Except what he saw. Blue wasn't squashed against the wall with his eyes rolling desperately. He wasn't curled up asleep with his head nestled between his front legs. He wasn't standing in the back of his stall, playfully pretending that he hadn't heard JoBob's call. He wasn't there at all.

JoBob's heart slammed against his rib bones. "Slim!" he yelled. "Where's Blue?" He looked around wildly, but Slim was nowhere to be seen. Then he spotted Gustavo through the open doors at the far end of the barn, mucking out the lesson-horse corral.

Running in the barn was strictly forbidden, but everything had gone out of JoBob's mind except Blue's safety. JoBob ran. "Gustavo," he yelled. "Where's

179

Slim? Where's Blue?"

"Over at the little barn, I think," Gustavo said, and JoBob whirled and ran back through the big barn the way he had come, past Blue's stall. Ex-stall, he supposed, because all of a sudden he'd figured it out. He stopped running. He almost laughed at himself for flying into such a panic. Slim had moved Blue to a different stall, that was all. But which one? Some of the panicky feeling was still with him and he needed to see Blue with his own eyes. To affirm that he was all right.

As soon as he stepped into the little barn he spotted Slim down at the other end, by the last stall in the aisle. The end of his morning rounds.

"Hi, JoBob," he called. "How you feelin'? Sure is nice to have you back." His usual affable voice, so that meant nothing was wrong with Blue. Everything was all right.

"Blue," JoBob blurted. "Where's Blue? Why did you move him?"

"Blue?" Slim looked puzzled and something in his voice made JoBob go cold all over. Something *was* wrong.

"Yes, Blue! Remember him? My horse. Where is he?"

"He's gone. I thought you knew."

"You mean he died? Or what? Gone where? *Gone?*"

"Calm down," Slim said. "He ain't dead."

"Then where is he? How would I know? Gone *where?*"

"To Santa Barbara. I sold him. Didn't your father tell you?"

JoBob didn't believe it. He opened his mouth and nothing came out. He stood stock-still, his head pounding, his ears ringing, and he saw Slim as if he were a very long way away. It was quiet in the barn, the usual sounds of horses shifting in their stalls, chewing their hay. It was a joke, JoBob decided. Slim's sense of humor could be a little strange sometimes. But his father? What did his father have to do with it?

"You're kidding me, right? But it's not funny. Where is he? You tell me right now. It's not funny, Slim!"

"I'm not kidding you. I sold him."

This time JoBob knew it was true. "He was *my* horse! You had no *right!*" yelling now. "You *sold* him? *Why?*"

"I thought you knew," Slim said, "but it's sure beginning to look like you didn't. Somethin' is screwy here. Ted Huggles, you know, the Blackstones' trainer, he called me up. Said he'd been watching Blue all during that Sacramento show and the more he saw, the better he liked him. So he offered big bucks, said they didn't need to try him, just ship him on down. But I said you was pretty attached to him and I wasn't so all-fired sure you'd want to sell him."

"Damn right I wouldn't!"

"I don't get it," Slim looked puzzled.

"I don't either!"

" 'Cause I called your house and talked to your father. He said he'd ask you. Then he comes over here and says you said it was okay, so I called up Ted and . . ."

JoBob thought he could never feel worse than he

had a few minutes ago when Slim told him Blue was gone. He was wrong. He felt a whole lot worse. "You *believed* him? You sold my horse without asking *me?*"

"Well, like I said, I was a mite surprised, but then I thought, shoot, you've got a good head on your shoulders. I've done a hell of a lot of horse tradin' and this was one of the sweetest deals I've ever done. When I said to Ted that I wasn't so sure you'd want to sell him, he upped the price by a thousand. I've been selling horses since way before you were born and no one ever offered to do *that* before." He stopped and mused. "Might try that line again . . ."

"You make me sick," JoBob said.

"Hang on. Simmer down. With money like that you can buy a couple of nice green horses, train 'em up, sell 'em. . . . Get you launched good in the horse trainin' business. Why, when I was your age I didn't even dream of having that much money. Don't you even want to know how much?"

"NO!" JoBob screamed. "Blue was *mine!* I don't give a tinker's damn about money. You stink just as bad as my father!" He was at Slim then, the tears licking hot in his eyes, his fists pounding at him, and his voice screaming and screaming: "No! No! No!"

"Hey now," Slim said. "Calm down." He caught JoBob's fists and turned him around so JoBob's back was against his chest, his arms holding JoBob tight. "I know you was fond of him. I was too. But he was a horse. That's what horses are for. Buy and sell . . ."

"No!" JoBob screamed. He kicked and writhed, trying to get away, trying to hurt Slim.

"Son, son," Slim said. "It ain't the end of the world."

"You don't know *nothin'*," JoBob spat. "Let me *go!*"

"Listen," Slim said, without loosening his grip, "If . . ."

"You shut up!" JoBob said. "And let me go. I never want to see you again as long as I live. Traitor! *Bastard!*"

"You watch your mouth," Slim said.

"No!" JoBob was kicking and screaming again, his mind reeling.

Slim tightened his grip and JoBob went limp. What was the use? Blue was gone.

"There now," Slim said. "Come on into the office and sit down for a spell. I'll get you a glass of water. If I'd known you felt so strongly I wouldn't have done it, but your father said you approved." Slim patted his shoulder. "I'm real sorry, JoBob."

JoBob couldn't stand to hear another word. He didn't believe Slim was sorry. If he was, how could he be standing there cool as a cucumber, smirking, and talking about what a sweet deal it was? JoBob whirled and ran. He ran around the big barn and into the pasture, across the pasture, stumbling over the rough plowed ground, running, tears streaming down his face, running. . . . He ran and ran and ran until he was gasping for air and he tasted blood in his throat. He threw himself down on the ground and pounded it with his fists, crying, shrieking, calling his father every name in the book, and then some. And Slim wasn't a whole lot better. Yammering on about money. It made JoBob want to puke. Money was just money, but Blue was . . . Blue was . . . Pictures of Blue started going in his head: Blue the way he'd looked the first day JoBob ever saw him, standing in the corner of the corral looking so bedraggled and forlorn; Blue with his coat shiny and his mane braided, arching his neck and stepping proudly when they went into the ring to pick up a ribbon; Blue with his cheery white face poked over the door of his stall whickering at JoBob when he came into the barn. How could he live without Blue?

JoBob's throat was raw, his shirt stuck to his skin, his face was streaked with tears and dirt, and inside he ached and ached. He cried and screamed, pounding his fist into the ground until finally, when he opened his mouth, all that came out was a croak. He'd screamed his voice away and it hadn't done any good. His heart felt like it had broken into a million pieces and every one of them hurt worse. . . .

After a long time he sat up and looked around. He realized with a shock that it was still morning. It seemed like years had passed since he'd walked into the barn that morning. He'd run all the way to the river. Three miles. The river where he and Trumaine used to come with Lulu and Blue. Where Blue would graze, his white socks and spots bright against the green of the grass. . . . *Used to come.* JoBob gave a strangled cry, but he was teared out. He'd cried all the tears in his body. But he was still crying inside. Blue was the only thing he'd ever owned. The only thing he'd ever loved. His *friend.* "Horses are to buy and sell," Slim had said, and remembering those words set him off again. He'd even admired Slim, wanted to be like him. Now Slim was the last person in the world he wanted to be like. He had a heart of stone. He thought the world was composed of dollars and cents. Not one bit different from his father. JoBob wished they would both fry in hell.

On the riverbank the willows blew gently in the wind, their branches long feathery fronds. JoBob wanted to bomb them. How dared those trees to be growing? How dared the sun to be shining? He had chores to do at the barn. He had Sophie to ride and Slim probably had a couple of others for him too, but he didn't care. He hoped the horses whose stalls he was supposed to muck were wallowing in manure, getting thrush, dying of founder. . . . He was never going back there again. Slim needed someone to ride any of those old nags, he could jolly well find someone else. It sure as hell wasn't going to be him.

JoBob rolled over onto his back and stared at the sun. You weren't supposed to look at the sun, it would fry your eyeballs. Fine. He didn't have any use for his eyes. His eyes edged toward the sun, but he couldn't make them look at it. His eyelids blinked no matter how hard he tried to make them stay open, and he pulled at them, trying to get them to behave.

Then he thought maybe it wasn't true. Maybe it was a dream—a horrible, horrible nightmare, and now it was time to wake up. He'd wake up and he'd get up, he'd go out the door of his house and he'd take the path through the woods with Flea capering along beside him and he'd go into the barn and he'd see Blue's face. He'd . . . No, he wouldn't. It was true. Blue was gone.

18

■ ■ ■

Toward evening JoBob's stomach told him
something he wouldn't have been absolutely sure about
if someone had asked him: he was alive. And he hadn't
had a thing to eat all day. He scrambled down the
riverbank, splashed his face with water, and took a
long drink. Then he got up and started home. Home
was about the last place he wanted to go, but he
couldn't think of anywhere else. It took all the energy
he had to pick up his left foot and put it down in
front of him. Then he had to pick up his right foot
and put *it* down in front of the left. Then it was
time for the left again. Seemed like it took him forever
to get home.

"Where you *been?*" his mother asked as soon as
he walked in the door. "Telephone's been ringing
off the hook all afternoon. Slim. Trumaine. 'Where's
JoBob?' they wanted to know. 'He all right?' Well,
why shouldn't you be all right? What's this all about?
How come you weren't at the barn?"

186

JoBob slumped into a chair and didn't bother to answer.

She stopped all of a sudden, walked over and laid her hand on his forehead. "You got a fever again? You don't look too good. You have a relapse? Oh dear, I shouldn't have let you go out so soon after that flu. Here, let me just get the thermometer, take your temperature." She was heading through the front room to the bathroom when JoBob said, "I'm not sick."

"Hm?"

"I said I'm not sick."

"What is it then? You're pale as a ghost."

JoBob sighed. He didn't want to talk about it, but he knew he'd have to sooner or later, so he might as well get it over with. "Blue got sold."

"You don't say!" She came back across the kitchen and sat down opposite JoBob. Darlene, with a sure instinct for bad timing, appeared at the door between the kitchen and the front room. "That's what those phone calls were about? Well, what's the deal? What do you mean he 'got sold'? Thought he was your horse."

Was. JoBob flinched and made himself answer, not looking at either of them. "He was. And I do mean 'got sold.' I sure as hell didn't do it. I'd *never* have sold Blue. Know who did it?"

"Well, Slim, I suppose, he . . ."

"No! Well, sort of. But who really did it was your husband, the son of a bitch."

"Now, JoBob, don't go talking about your father like that."

"And don't start giving me any of that 'honor thy

father' crap either," JoBob yelled. "Did you hear what I said? Don't you get what he did? He stole my horse, and then he sold him."

"Stole?"

Darlene giggled. "Sounds pretty dramatic. Did he sneak into the barn in the middle of the night? Like those cattle rustlers on 'Gunsmoke'?"

"Oh, for God's sake, Darlene."

"And sold him to some fancy dude in L.A. for a hundred thousand dollars, and then, they find out that it was a shady deal and they come after him. They come here in one of those long sleek limos, four guys in black suits, with hats, you know, and submachine guns like Al Capone. . . . No! Like Jesse James. They figure it out, see, they find out that you were this poor little orphan boy and the only thing you had in the whole world was that horse and they realize that you've been done dirty too, so they come in search of . . . They come for retribution and, oh! Oh no! They see me. They say, 'Now there's a cute little piece,' and they kidnap me. They take me to their yacht. It's one of those huge white ones registered in some fake country so it can never be traced and . . ."

JoBob blanked out. What a family. Next thing he knew, his mother was saying, "Darlene, you cut it out. Nobody stole anything. You're just as bad as the rest of 'em."

She got up and went over to the Frigidaire. Took out a bunch of carrots and a head of lettuce and a cucumber. "Now you come help me with supper, and, JoBob, you go wash up. You look a fright."

188

She carried the vegetables over to the sink and JoBob got up and followed her.

"Mom, if I took Pop's truck to town and sold it, what would you call that?"

"Oh . . . Well . . . Now you didn't do that, did you?"

"No! But that's what he did!"

"He wouldn't do a thing like that. He knew how attached you were to that horse." She scraped hard at the carrot with the peeler, like maybe, if she got away enough carrot peel, she'd be getting a lot of other things away too.

JoBob didn't know why he was even bothering to talk to her. Of course she wouldn't believe that Gavin did anything bad—at least not if JoBob said so. "Okay, you don't believe it, why don't you ask him? Where is he, anyway?"

"Oh, I don't know. Down at Riley's, I suppose."

Then JoBob thought of something else. While he was sick he'd stayed in his room, sleeping, reading, listening to the radio, hadn't paid much attention to what was going in the rest of the house. His room was tiny and it was hot under the eaves, but it was his and he'd enjoyed the peacefulness of it without the uproars that went on when his father was around. Now he remembered that he hadn't heard any of those. One evening his father had gotten out the accordion and sat on the front porch singing, which he hadn't done for a long, long time. "Tell me what kind of mood he's been in for the last few days."

"Uh, well . . ."

"He's been in a great mood," Darlene chimed in.

"He even gave me ten dollars. Told me to go get something nice for myself. I've never been so surprised in my life. And I heard him talkin' to Chet. Said somethin' about a plum falling into his lap."

"Bought himself a new suit, too," his mother said, and the peeler in her hand slowed down.

"See?" JoBob asked. "Since when did he ever offer to give anybody money? Where do you think he got it?"

"Well, I don't know. You know I don't pry into . . ."

Just then JoBob heard a truck on the road. The unmistakable clickety-clank of Gavin's truck with the lifters rattling. It would take him about twenty minutes to adjust those lifters, but he never bothered.

Then he burst in the door singing, "Summertime, and the livin' is easy. Fish are jumpin' and the cotton is high . . ." filling up the whole room with his big body, his black hair flying in a shock over his forehead, whirling around and swaying his shoulders to the rhythm of the song.

His mother turned and snapped, "Why is it so easy, all of a sudden?" You could have knocked JoBob over with a feather. Usually when his father was in one of these happy moods she fell right in with it.

Gavin stopped singing. He stood still in the middle of the room. "What's got into *you?*" He glared at the three of them as if they surprised him in some way, as if he'd expected some other situation—or people—altogether. "What's going on here? Beautiful spring day and you three just standin' there like bumps on a log."

No one said anything. He smiled and shrugged.

"You all want to be sad sacks, fine. But me . . . 'Gonna have some real music now." He went into the front room, humming "Summertime."

In the front room the opening strains of "Shall We Dance" came from the Victrola. When the prelude was over, he came back into the kitchen, singing along with Yul Brynner: "Shall we dance? On a bright cloud of music shall we fly? Shall we dance? Shall we then . . ." He waltz-stepped up to the sink and laid his hand on Cerise's. Took the peeler out of her hand and pulled her toward him.

"May I have this dance, Mrs. Draper?"

"Oh, Gavin, I've got supper to get."

"It can wait. It's Saturday night, baby. Come on!"

He danced her around the room, singing. Then, when the singing stopped, and the music swept into the orchestral part, he dipped and soared as if he'd never taken a lame step in his life. *She* was dancing too. Her skirt twirled gracefully around her legs and she held her head high, gazing over Gavin's shoulder, and looking all at the same time faraway, dreamy, pleased. Then she turned and looked into Gavin's eyes with the same expression. She looked almost as young as Darlene. Then the reprise—with Gavin singing again: "Or perchance—when the last little star has left the sky, shall we still be together with our arms around each other, and . . ."

JoBob went into the front room and took the needle off the record. He couldn't believe it. *Dancing.* Letting on like nothing had happened. No, letting on like there was something to celebrate. It made him want to puke.

Gavin came to the door. "What'd you do that for?"

"You know," JoBob said. He knew he was taking a chance. His father didn't like to be crossed—especially not when he was in one of his good moods. He could lash out quick, but JoBob was way beyond caring what happened to his body. Gavin didn't yell, or come at him, though. He backed into the kitchen and sat down on one of the kitchen chairs.

"What do I know?" he asked, with no inflection at all.

JoBob stood in the doorway with one hand on either side of the door frame. He needed some help to keep on standing up. His mother dropped into a chair too, and Darlene half-turned from where she stood by the sink, one hand on her hip, her eyes moving around, scanning the three of them.

"JoBob says you sold his horse," Cerise said. "That true?"

Gavin cleared his throat, opened his mouth, then shut it again.

It was dead quiet in the kitchen.

Then, "No. I wouldn't do such a thing."

"You're lying." JoBob's voice was dead quiet too. "Slim said that you . . ."

"Oh, Mr. Fancy Abbott, huh? You puttin' the word of that Texas tinhorn against your own father?"

"Yes! *He's* not a liar. Or a thief, either."

"By God, I've had enough of your lip." Gavin started out of his chair and JoBob stood quite still in the doorway, watching his father's hands resting on the tabletop, palms flat, the muscles of his forearms hard and flexed, his torso half out of the chair. Maybe this time his father was going to kill him. JoBob waited, not moving at all, feeling strangely peaceful. He didn't care. He just flat-ass didn't care.

"Wait a minute," Cerise said. "Where'd you get the money you gave Darlene? Where'd you get the money to buy that new suit?"

Gavin dropped back into his chair, looking puzzled, then surprised; then crafty. "Oh well, little opportunity just happened along. You don't need to worry your pretty little head about it."

"You stop it, Gavin. Did you sell his horse? Or not?"

"Yes!" he yelled. "So what's the big deal?"

"It was *his*, that's what. You had no right. Stealing from your own son."

JoBob couldn't believe it. His mother taking his side instead of his father's.

Gavin blustered, "Oh come, come. I just sort of borrowed it. Way I look at it, this here's a family and we all help each other out."

"*You* never did a thing to help out. Now you give him the money. It's bad enough to go sneaking around, selling his horse, and then . . ."

Gavin seemed to get smaller, sagging down into his chair, his shoulders drooping and his chin nearly on his chest. "I can't."

"Why not?"

"I don't have it."

"You don't have it? Flora was telling me that horse was worth a thousand dollars at least. What in God's name did you spend that kind of money on?"

"Now look here, baby, I didn't want you to worry, but I got into a little spot of trouble at that fight over in Grass Valley. That's a pretty tough crowd and I was backed into a real tight corner and . . . Between a rock and a hard place, believe you me, but then this plum drops into my lap, and . . ." His voice was low, almost a whine.

His mother used to say he could talk the leaves off a tree. Now it looked like she knew him too well. He was talking and talking and she was sitting there, listening, looking like she didn't believe a word he said. JoBob was disgusted. He was more than disgusted. He had this horrible empty, achy place inside where Blue used to be. But with another part of him, he was enjoying it. His mother was finally figuring it out. Then he thought about the money. What he'd said to Slim about the money was only partly true, he now realized. He wanted Blue a whole lot more than he wanted any money, but now it looked like he didn't have that either. His father had taken everything he had. He had nothing.

Gavin changed his tone again. "It's his fault anyway," he said belligerently, glaring at JoBob. "If he'd come to help me like he was supposed to, none of this would have happened. I had a real good scam going, and then he ups and . . ."

"You just wanted him to do your dirty work," Cerise said. "And I'm thankful somebody around here knows the difference between right and wrong."

"You shut up!" Gavin swore. Then a lot of things happened at once: he got up so fast his chair tipped over backward with a crash, he stomped over to the door; at the same time Cerise jumped up too, and *she* was yelling, in a way that JoBob had never heard

194

before, like she was really angry, like she really meant it, this time. She followed him out onto the back porch and for awhile the yelling continued. Then their voices dropped down to a murmur and JoBob figured his father had won again—sweet-talked his mother around to his side.

At the sink Darlene turned on the faucet and started washing lettuce.

Outside Gavin's truck started, backfired, died. Started again and screeched off down the road. JoBob went into the front room and sat down on the sofa. It was one of the first times in his life he could remember being in that room by himself, and without the TV on. He looked at the blank screen. It told him nothing. The grandmother clock, which his mother had brought with her from Virginia, swung its pendulum back and forth, a ticking so faint you could hardly hear it. JoBob heard it. "Nothing, nothing," it said as it swung back and forth.

19
■■■

E<small>VER SINCE</small> he'd started riding, JoBob had had more to do in most days than he had time for. Now, day after day, he'd open his eyes in the morning and wonder why he should get up. If he could sleep all twenty-four hours it might be bearable until . . . until what? He could see all the rest of the days of his life stretching on and on and on like telephone poles along the highway. Dark, solitary, the next one no different from the one before. Downstairs, he'd hear the clatter of his mother and Darlene getting breakfast in the kitchen. Then his mother would be calling up the stairs for him to get up. He got up. He put on his clothes and, if he had time, he ate his breakfast; if he didn't, he went on to school without it. Eating seemed like a dumb thing to do anyway. Sometimes he sat in his classes at school. Other times he cut. School seemed more pointless than ever.

After school he went to the barn, and that was the worst part of the day because it made him miss Blue the most. He rode Sophie and mucked his stalls and cleaned his tack. Slim had sold Twinkle and had a new green horse named Choo-choo that he wanted JoBob to ride. JoBob said he'd rather not. Instead of stretching out the afternoons at the barn like he used to, he'd leave as soon as he'd done his work. He'd go through the woods toward home and when he got within sight of the house he circled around to the front. If his father's truck was there, he'd go back around through the woods and call Flea. If his father's truck was gone, he'd go inside and turn on the TV. He didn't want to risk running into his father any more than he had to. Funny thing was, his father didn't seem to want to be around him, either. He spent way more time away from home than he used to, doing what, JoBob didn't know.

JoBob would turn on the TV and watch for hours, totally absorbed, but afterward didn't remember what any of the characters had done or said. He didn't even remember what shows he'd been watching—which was just part of what was happening to him. His mind was turning to mush, he figured, but he considered that with the same kind of objectivity he had when deciding whether to put on a blue shirt or a plaid one. It didn't seem to matter much.

There was always a point, though, when a little voice in his head whispered: this show is stupid, JoBob. He'd ignore it and stare at the TV, trying to get involved again, but the people on the screen had gone nonsensical. So he turned off the TV, turned on the radio.

Earth angel, earth angel, the one I adore
Love you forever and ever mo-ore . . .

He switched it off. *Nothing* was forever. Except dying.

When he could no longer be distracted by the radio or the TV, he'd go outside. Flea knew there was something wrong with him. At first she'd tried to cajole him. She'd bring him sticks and tried to get him to play fetch with her, but he wouldn't do it. So she stopped trying to play. When he came outside she greeted him the way she always did, wagging her tail and whimpering with pleasure when he hunkered down beside her and scratched her ears. But there the old way ended. JoBob shoved his hands into his pockets and walked off into the woods. Sometimes, when he cut school, he spent the whole day in the woods. He walked and walked, with no plan or direction in mind. He just walked. Other times he didn't have the energy to walk. He'd lie down on the ground and stare up into the trees for hours, watching the leaves moving lightly against the sky. Flea always came with him, padding along right beside him. She didn't go bounding off after squirrels and birds like she used to. When he stopped, she dropped down beside him a foot or so away, laid her head on her front paws and never took her eyes off him, as if she thought that by keeping him in her sight she was insuring that he was all right.

Sometimes JoBob didn't go far, just to the copse past the chicken runs, where he'd made a ball trap out of an old tire and a tarp. He'd take his baseball and throw it for hours. When he was in a baseball mood Flea perked up considerably. For the first hour or so she'd retrieve the ball for him. Then she'd flop down and go to sleep. Those were the only times when she was with him that she went to sleep. As if she trusted the baseball to keep him safe. JoBob didn't love baseball the way Trumaine did, but he found it satisfying to throw the ball as hard as he could. It landed in the trap with a satisfying "thwack" and he imagined that the trap was his father's face and the ball was a dumdum that exploded when it made contact, blowing the face to smithereens.

Something strange happened to time. Sometimes it would seem to stand still, a few seconds stretched out and out so he believed that he would hang in that moment forever, caught in permanent suspension. Never again would time move forward. Other times there were whole hours and days that passed, he knew—the date changed on the newspaper—but he had no memory of them. It was the same with people and things. Some things were so clear and sharp they were lodged indelibly in his mind: a spider web in the corner of his room, the filaments strong and gossamer, or the branch of a tree outlined against the sky, or two little boys crouched in a vacant lot in town, playing marbles; but the people who were familiar to him drifted through his space pale and insubstantial as smoke. At night he did not dream.

One afternoon Slim said, "Say, JoBob, Mel told me about a gelding up in Auburn. Said he was real attractive. Liver chestnut. We could go take a look at him. Might be a good replacement for Blue. . . ."

"No." JoBob said.

"Oh, come on," Slim said. "You know Mel knows a good horse when he sees one and the price is right. You and me could be partners. Go halfsies. I'll buy him and you work with him. You're gettin' a reputation now—because of Blue—just the other day Red calls me up, asks if I've got any other stock along those lines. So . . . If this horse is anything like as good as I think, it wouldn't take long. We could turn him over pretty fast, make some good money, and . . ."

"I don't want to make good money," JoBob said. "And I'm never buying another horse. Get the picture?"

Slim shook his head and looked sad. "You'll never be a trainer, then. Buyin' and sellin' is the only way to make good money. Lessons and the other stuff is just peanuts."

"So what?"

"Can't live on air," Slim said.

JoBob didn't answer and Slim walked away. Then he snapped his fingers and turned back, looking a lot different—excited, almost. "I just had an idea. You don't want to do no deals, you could go to the track. Why, I was just talkin' to Eddie Elwood—you remember him? Come up a few months ago in between meets. He's a trainer—down at Hollywood Park, right now. He said they was . . ."

"Tryin' to get rid of me?" JoBob snapped.

"No. No. If you was to go, I'd miss you. Just seems to me it might be good for you to have a change of scene, and you could be of use at the track. Not many kids your size, and sure as hell not many with your hands and feel for a horse. Trainers'd be standin' in line beggin' you to ride for them."

"Yeah, sure." JoBob didn't believe a word of it.

Slim changed then, his face dark with anger, madder

than JoBob had ever seen him. He came up real close to JoBob and shook his finger in his face. "You better change your tune, buster. Notice what side of your bread the butter's on. You keep bitin' the hand that feeds you, you'll be sorry as hell one of these days. *Real* sorry." Then he stepped back a yard or two, took off his hat, and mopped his face with his handkerchief.

"I know you're grievin', but you've got to get over it some time." This time his voice was quiet, kind.

"No, I don't." That's what his mother said too. She said it wasn't natural for a boy his age to go moping around like that.

"Suit yourself," Slim said in the flattest voice JoBob had ever heard coming from him. Like Slim didn't care anymore. Then Slim turned and walked out of the barn.

JoBob hung the last bridle he had to clean on the tack hook. Fine. He didn't care, either. He swabbed at the saddle soap with the sponge and pulled it over the bridle fast and furiously. Then he slung the bridle into the tack room and headed for home, walking fast, Slim's voice rocketing around in his head: "Make some good money . . . a replacement for Blue . . ." A *replacement* for Blue. Just hearing the word made him sick. It also made him angrier than he was already. More violent. He ran home, and when he got to the baseball trap he grabbed his baseball and threw it and threw it and threw it. The ball was smashing Slim to smithereens. It was smashing Mel and his father and the gelding in Auburn. . . . And then . . . he sat down and cried. He couldn't believe it. Before Blue left, he couldn't remember crying. Ever. Now he was turning into a regular old crybaby. Some kind of sissy who might as well take to wearing skirts and putting his hair up in curlers. But he didn't care.

Flea came and licked the tears off his face. "You don't care either, do you?" he asked. "And I know you won't tell."

It kept on like that. He still had to do his chores at home, and he did them; but it was the same as when he was at the barn or at school: almost as if someone else was doing these things while JoBob himself had gone to some point in the distance—about treetop level—and was watching the JoBob body mix the chicken feed, ride a horse, sit in class, put a forkful of food into his mouth. . . .

Then it was June. School was over and everyone at the barn was getting ready to go to the Siskiyou County Fair Horse Show up in Yreka. JoBob remembered how he'd been looking forward to that show, how he'd decided that he and Blue were on a roll, and . . . It was like some other person had had those feelings. Not anyone JoBob could recognize now. He told Slim he didn't want to go to the show.

"But I'm countin' on you to ride Sophie."

JoBob shook his head. "Let K.T. ride her. Or Trumaine. I'm not going."

Slim shook *his* head. Then JoBob noticed something, and it seemed like the first thing he'd noticed in about a hundred years. Slim looked concerned. He looked worried.

"I . . . I'm sorry," JoBob said, "but I *can't* go.

202

B—" He stopped and bit his lip. He was going to say Blue might be there. And he couldn't stand the idea of seeing him. Of seeing Celia Blackstone riding his horse. But if he even said Blue's name he'd cry, and cry in front of Slim he would not do. He had some pride left.

He took a deep breath and said, "I'll stay here and help out Gustavo, okay? I'll ride any horses you want. Even that old Auburn gelding." Slim had bought the gelding Mel had seen over in Auburn. The day he arrived at the barn Slim had tried once more to get JoBob to take an interest, and JoBob nearly lost his temper. He didn't, though—just told Slim he wasn't going to ride him that day or any other, and to please not ask him to. Since then Slim hadn't mentioned it.

Now Slim cracked a grin. "Okay, son. I sure appreciate it. Ain't no one around here has the feel for a greenie you do."

JoBob smiled back, and that was another thing he hadn't done in a long time.

Slim patted him on the shoulder, and when he started down the barn aisle on his evening rounds he looked a lot more sprightly than he had in quite awhile.

JoBob was glad he wasn't going to the show. He really was scared about what he might do if he saw Celia riding Blue, but he was glad that he'd thought of something to help Slim out, too. He was still hurt that Slim had sold Blue. No, Slim had just been sort of an agent. His father had really done it. If it weren't for him, he would still have Blue. He'd be going to the show, he'd be riding Blue in the medals and hunt-ers, maybe even try a jumper class or two, see what Blue could do over those courses that were a lot harder and were a real test of a horse's ability. He'd . . .

JoBob was still working for Slim, so he helped pack for the Yreka show. He sorted tack, stacked buckets, and loaded trunks. When all the gear was packed he brought out the horses one by one for Slim to load into the van. The familiar going-to-a-show routine. Only it wasn't familiar. Because this time Blue wasn't in the van and, instead of climbing into the cab with Slim and heading down the road full of anticipation about the show, JoBob stood outside the barn, waving. Slim tooted the horn, JoBob waved again, and then the van was gone.

After they left, the barn seemed empty and strange. Never before had JoBob spent more than one day at the barn without Slim being there too. Most of the horses had gone with Slim, so there wasn't a whole lot of work to do. JoBob rode Choo-choo and the gelding from Auburn in the morning, while it was still cool, riding them the way he'd done everything since Blue had left. Without paying a whole lot of attention. Then he took off in the afternoons roaming through the woods with Flea.

20
■■■

O N F RIDAY of that week it turned hot. The
first day that year that had been real summer hot.
On Saturday, JoBob woke up early and it was already
so hot he could tell it was going to be a real scorcher.
So he decided to leave the horses until evening and
spend the day down by the river. He was seized with
a desire to go swimming that had more to it than
the heat. He wanted to feel the water on his body,
the softness of it on his skin, like a caress. He wanted
to float in the water and watch the little swallows
darting and skimming above him in graceful spins
and swoops nearly as quick as the small insects they
caught in midair. There was more to it than that,
even, but he couldn't quite put it into words. Maybe
he'd find out when he got there.

The place he was thinking about was miles farther
upstream than the one he and Trumaine used to go
to with Blue and Lulu. It was at a bend in the river
where the main current swung out in a wide arc,

leaving a deep quiet pool nestled in the crook of a bluff. It didn't have a grapevine swing like the place near the barn, and it wasn't a very good fishing place either, so he was pretty sure he'd be alone there.

He packed a lunch and said, "Come on, Flea, today we're going to the river."

She barked happily and they set off through the woods. He liked the friendly green canopy of the trees overhead and the way the light filtered through, dappling the leaves and twigs on the ground.

After two hours of brisk walking JoBob came to a spot where the woods opened into a wide grassy meadow that sloped up to the bluff above the bend in the river. A lone oak stood a little way out in the meadow, as if it couldn't decide whether it belonged in the woods or the open. It was a huge live oak with a trunk much bigger around than two or three of him could circle with their hands. The grandfather of the woods, he decided. On one of the lower branches JoBob spotted a speckled hawk, his spots blending perfectly with the dappling of the light and the leaves. JoBob motioned Flea down with his hand and decided to wait as long as the hawk was there. The hawk sat very still except for his head, which swiveled first in one direction, then another, so quickly JoBob sometimes wasn't sure that he *had* turned his head. He caught sight of JoBob and ruffled the feathers along his back, half-unfolded his wings. Then he seemed to decide that JoBob was not threatening. He folded his wings again and went back to perusing the country-side. JoBob watched him for a long time, locked in some timeless space that was just hawk and him. Then

206

the hawk was off, with a swift whir of wingbeat, and soon he was soaring high, high across the meadow. JoBob wished he could take off like that hawk. The way he used to do in dreams, the way he used to do on Blue.

"Oh well," he said to Flea, "come on, let's go swimming."

Flea jumped up and trotted out into the meadow as if she knew perfectly well where they were going.

JoBob started after her, but something made him look down. At his feet lay three long tail feathers mottled gray, white, black. He decided they were a sign of some kind, a gift the hawk-spirit had sent him. He stood very still, trying to get his mind to slow down to hawk time, to find out what the message was. He stood like that a long time, waiting. . . . Flea came back and gave him a questioning bark. "All right," JoBob said, "maybe I'll get it later." Then he picked up the feathers and started across the meadow, with Flea capering ahead of him, certain that he was coming now too.

At the crest of the bluff she stopped suddenly and froze. Had she spotted a coon? Not likely at midday, but coons were unpredictable and he'd seen coon tracks there before. JoBob quickened his step until he stood beside her where he could see the river.

It wasn't a coon, but a girl. A girl in Levi's and a pink shirt crouched by the river, looking down into the water. JoBob was so mad he wanted to throw something at her, or sic Flea on her. He hadn't come all this way to have his space taken over by some girl.

"Well, that tears it," he said to Flea. "Let's go." And he turned to go back into the woods, but Flea barked furiously at him, ran headlong down the bank, and plunged into the river.

Damn dog. She could be good as gold when it suited her. But not when it counted. Like now.

He stood on the bluff, looking at the river, at the girl and his dog, trying to decide what to do. Now he couldn't even go swimming. He hadn't brought a bathing suit because he'd expected to be alone.

She stood up and waved.

He'd been so angry to find anyone there that it hadn't occurred to him he might know her. But he did. It was Mariko.

JoBob scrambled down the bank and when he reached the bottom he said, "What are you doing here? It's a long way from home."

She smiled, looking straight at him. "I came to fish," she said, "and to . . ." Her expression changed, as if she were about to say something else more important. But she didn't, simply asked, "What about you?"

"I was going to swim. Have lunch," he said angrily. How could he go swimming now? "This is a lousy place to fish. Much better down at Carson's Landing."

"I know, but it's peaceful here. And what's important about fishing is not whether or not you catch anything."

"Could have fooled me," JoBob said. "I thought the *point* of fishing was catching fish."

"Only if you look at it that way." She looked at the river, then back at him. Not smiling, or frowning. Just looking at him the way she'd done last—When was it when he'd met her in the woods? Seemed like

208

about a hundred years ago. He looked back at her and then he felt himself blushing.

"Did you see that hawk?" he asked, turning toward the meadow, so she wouldn't notice him blushing.

"Yes," she said. "I was trying to decide what it would be like to be a hawk. To be able to fly so free. . . ."

"I was thinking the same thing," he said. "I saw him back in the woods, sitting in that big oak. He left these . . . for you. Here."

What did he do that for? He'd been planning to keep those feathers for himself. They were important.

She took the feathers and brushed them lightly back and forth in her hand, then she set them down beside her and took them up one at a time, holding each one at arm's length and looking at it. "Aren't these colors amazing? See how the black only *looks* black. And the white too. It's really all gray, but not the way you think of gray. Bleak and dreary." She put them in the basket by her side and said, "Thank you very much."

JoBob sat down not too close, but he could smell her. The same fresh and outdoorsy smell he'd noticed before. "Gathering mushrooms?" he asked, nodding toward the basket.

"No. No mushrooms in summer. Only in the rainy season."

"Oh. Well," he said, "I . . . uh . . . I was going to have some lunch. Want some?"

"No thank you."

"I can't eat with you sitting there looking at me like that."

"I won't look, then," she said and promptly turned

ninety degrees, so when he turned his head he was looking at her back.

He opened the sack and took out his sandwich. He sat holding the sandwich in his hand, looking at her straight back and her hair like a curtain of black silk. The shirt, he noticed, wasn't solid pink, but teeny stripes.

JoBob crawled around in a half-circle so he was facing her again. "Come on," he said, extending half the sandwich to her. "I can't eat looking at your back either."

"I *am* hungry," she said, "but I didn't want to rob you of your lunch."

"I've got plenty." This wasn't strictly true. He only had a baloney sandwich, an apple, and some cookies, but she was so . . . so *polite* that he knew he had to make her believe it.

She said thank you and took the half sandwich from him. When they finished the sandwich, JoBob cut the apple in two with his pocket knife and gave her half.

Flea came bounding out of the river and when she was just close enough to get them wet, shook herself, spraying them both with water. They jumped up and ran off a pace or two. Flea came right with them and shook herself again.

JoBob wished that Flea would have better manners, but Mariko was laughing. He laughed too. Then Flea flopped down and went to sleep.

They sat down again and ate the cookies. JoBob crumpled up the paper bag and stuck it in his pocket. Now what? He felt like he ought to do or say something,

210

but he couldn't think of a thing. He looked at Flea. Then at the river. Then at Mariko. She was looking at him too. The hawk soared back overhead. Flea made little dreaming noises in her sleep. The water in the river slipped past with a faint gurgle. JoBob thought of the Navajo story again. It sure hadn't worked that day he'd gone over to her house, but it might work now. Especially since they were outdoors and it was just the two of them.

He didn't have a pipe, but maybe the hawk feathers would do. Or the breeze soughing through the trees. He was thinking how nice it was to see her again—like this—without all the other things getting in the way.

"It's nice to see you," Mariko said at last.

"It's nice to see you too," JoBob said, thinking that it did work, after all. "How come you've been avoiding me?"

She looked down. "I thought you were avoiding *me*."

"No. Well, not you in particular. Just . . . Oh, everybody, pretty much."

"Oh. I thought it *was* me in particular and . . ." She caught her lower lip between her teeth and looked down. A tear was running down her cheek. Then another one.

Oh God, now what? Crying girls made him nervous as hell. "Cut it out," he said. "Don't do that." He thought about slapping her—not hard enough to hurt, just enough to knock some sense into her. He'd heard that was the only way to reach a hysterical person. But she wasn't hysterical—at least he didn't think she was—she was crying, that's all. She raised her eyes and they were dark and liquid and beseeching, like . . . like Blue's.

"Hey," he said softly, "it's all right. Don't. Please? I never thought . . . I mean, I didn't mean to hurt your feelings, I really didn't."

"It's okay," she said wiping her cheeks with the back of her hand. "I guess you didn't. Sometimes I thought something was wrong with you, you looked, uh, kind of lost, but then you were so standoffish, I thought it was something I did, so . . ."

"Nothin' you did," he muttered.

"Somebody else, then? Did something bad happen?"

"Yes." Then he was telling her about Blue, and his father, and Slim, and how awful he felt. How no one knew how much it hurt. How they just kept telling him he should get over it. He went on for quite a long while, the words tumbling out in a rush, saying things that he'd never told anyone.

She didn't interrupt or ask questions or make any comments. She simply listened, and the more she listened the more he talked.

Finally, he'd said it all. He stopped.

She put her hand on his. "How awful. I'm really sorry." Simple words, but the way she said them made him feel better. It also made him want to cry. And, oh Lord, then he was crying. Not crying and shrieking the way he'd done before, just tears running down his cheeks, and it felt almost good, like a relief. Funny, though; he didn't mind doing it in front of her.

She squeezed his hand and he noticed how soft hers was. He squeezed it back. "Thank you."

"For what? I didn't do anything."

212

"Yes, you did. You listened. And . . . and you understand. I think?"

"I . . . well, I know what it's like to lose something—someone you're real fond of. To feel like no one else knows. Or cares."

JoBob was astounded. "Oh, what? Could you tell me? I mean . . ."

She did something with her head that could have been a no or a yes. Then she took her hand away from his and brushed her hair back. JoBob thought she was going to tell him right then. He wondered what it was, and he hoped she was going to.

"And you don't end up with nothing," she said in a low, musing voice. "I have—you have this. The river, the sky, hawk feathers . . . And you have the memories. No one can take those away."

She was right. Up until now he hadn't liked the memories. They were too painful, they made him miss Blue too much, but now he thought of the good times. He did have some wonderful memories and just then they didn't hurt. What if he'd never had Blue at all? Then he wouldn't even have the memories.

"Seems to me you have something else, too."

"What?"

"Knowledge, skill. Didn't you learn a lot from Blue?"

"Yes."

"No one can take that away either. Can they?"

"No."

She reached for her basket and got up.

He jumped up too. "Hey, you're not leaving are you? I thought . . . I thought . . . You're not going to fish?"

"I already have, and if you want to swim . . ."

213

"Why don't you come swimming too?" he blurted and immediately wished he hadn't, because what if she said yes? She'd take off all her clothes and he would see her . . . her breasts, which he noticed right then moving up and down underneath her blouse. And . . . and he'd see the rest of her . . . body, and he would die if she did that, because the mere thought of it got him excited. He couldn't cross his legs or put something in front of him, so he just stood there hoping, *praying* that she hadn't noticed. Thinking at the same time that it was a good thing she was so polite, because he didn't think she'd look at him there . . .

"I don't know how."

"Wh-what?"

"I don't know how."

"Oh."

"And it's getting late. My parents will worry if I'm not home on time."

She was right. It was getting late and he still had two horses to ride. "Well, maybe we could do this again?"

She smiled. "I would like that." Then she was off.

214

21
∎∎∎

J o Bob wanted to walk back home with Mariko. It would have been doing two sides of a triangle, and walking the extra distance he didn't mind a bit. Trouble was, he didn't have time. He let Flea come with him, which he usually didn't do. Slim didn't like a bunch of extra dogs at the barn. But Slim wasn't there, and maybe Flea would behave, for a change, that day. She wouldn't chase the horses or attack the barn cats. It was four-thirty and still plenty hot, but by the time he got to the barn it would be close to six and cooling off some. "It's been a good day, so far," he told Flea as they walked along. "Not what I planned on, but a lot better, really. A *lot* better," he repeated, remembering Mariko's voice and the way she looked at him. The way her hand had felt in his. The way she *was*.

He wanted to do a lot more than walk home with her. He wanted to spend more time with her, find out more about who she was, and have her find out more about who he was. He hated to think that she thought he'd been mad at her. He stopped and picked up a stick and threw it for Flea. Her tongue was lolling with the heat, but when she saw him pick up the stick she jumped up in the air yelping with excitement, and was after it, running fast. JoBob smiled. He guessed he'd been sort of mean to Flea, too.

When he got to the barn he rode Choo-choo first. He was real stiff to the left and he had a terrible mouth, so JoBob did a lot of bending exercises with him. He'd been doing those all week. Now he noticed that he'd softened considerably. He was bending correctly, with his body in a true arc, the center of which was JoBob's left leg—when he was bending to the left—while JoBob's right leg kept his hindquarters from swinging out too far to the right and his hands kept his head and shoulders on the arc. When he was bending like that his mouth softened up too.

Since Blue had been gone JoBob had been riding Sophie, but he'd been doing it the same way he'd been doing everything else. From a real faraway place where it didn't make any impression on him. Now he started to be aware of his body again. He felt his seat bones in the saddle, his legs on the side of the horse, his heels sinking down deep in the stirrups, his fingers on the reins. He *liked* to ride, he thought with surprise, as if he'd never thought it before.

Then he went to get the gelding from Auburn. He didn't have any particular problems, he was just ignorant. JoBob had been doing real basic stuff with him on the flat—simple transitions like trot-walk-halt, two speeds at the trot, wide easy turns. It had been

216

awhile since JoBob had ridden a horse this green and it reminded him of how it had been with Blue in the beginning. *Blue.* The pain pierced him, sharp as a knife wound, hurting as much as it ever had.

JoBob dropped the reins and Auburn stopped, swiveling his ears back as if to say, "What's going on?" JoBob folded his arms over his chest, trying to contain it, make it better somehow. He didn't know how long he sat like that. A minute? Five minutes? Then it was over. "I'll be damned," JoBob said to himself. Is this what they meant? His mother and Slim, when they said he'd get over it. Before, he thought they meant he'd get over it, forget it, like it never happened. Now he thought something different.

That maybe it *was* like a terrible wound. When it first happens, it bleeds, it hurts so bad you can't think of anything else. Then it begins to heal. It stops hurting and finally it does heal, but you always have the scar. If you get hit on that scar in a certain way, then you get a flash of the old pain as sharp and painful as it was in the first place. The pain passes more quickly, though, and the wound goes back to being a scar. It becomes a part of you, and you almost appreciate it—because you have something other people don't. You look at people who have never been hurt like that, and you almost feel sorry for them. They're like desk soldiers who have never been out on the battlefield. Never had to face fire and so they never know what kind of stuff they're made of. . . .

Auburn stamped and nudged at the bit. "Be patient," JoBob told him. "Rider is recovering from emotion." Flea sat up from her spot by the half-round

217

jump in the middle of the ring and barked a question. "No, Flea," JoBob said. "I'm not finished yet." While he was riding, she lay in the shade of the half-round. Then, when he went into the barn to change horses, she came along with him. She barked again, as if she knew something else was going on. A little breeze stirred through the leaves of the big oak in front of the barn. Birds twittered and chirped. Far off in the distance a train hooted.

JoBob took a deep breath. "Okay, Buddy," he said to Auburn. "That one has passed. Now let's see what you can do over these fences." He picked up the reins and trotted around to the fences he'd set earlier. Up until now he'd worked him over poles on the ground and jumped some little Xs. This evening JoBob had decided he was ready for something more challenging, so he'd made a gymnastic of four trot poles to an X, then one stride to another X. All simple, actually, and things he'd already done. The challenge was for him to put them together instead of doing them one at a time. Auburn pricked his ears on the approach, then went right through it, jumping pretty good for a green horse. Nothing like as awkward as Sophie had been at first. JoBob patted him and told him he was a good boy. Auburn cocked an ear back, waiting for the next signal from JoBob. Slim had been right about this horse. He *was* pretty nice for just your regular old garden variety horse. JoBob worked him through the gymnastic several more times, then patted him and took him back to the barn.

He put Auburn away, thinking that Slim would be pleased with the way he was going. JoBob closed his stall door and stood outside for a minute, watching him chew his hay. Then he heard Slim's voice, so clearly he might have been standing right there instead of it being a memory. "I'm sorry," Slim had said. "If I'd known how upset you was going to be, I wouldn't have sold him." At the time JoBob had been so upset, he didn't believe him. Hardly even *heard* him. He'd pasted onto Slim—and a lot of other people too—the anger he had for his father. He still had that. He knew his father wasn't sorry, but he now believed that Slim was. He also started remembering—really getting it, now—how kind Slim had been since. Trying to get him to take an interest. Suggesting that job at the track.

Maybe he would do it. Why not? Funny how things you thought were a disadvantage—like being small—could turn out to be an advantage. If he were as tall as K.T. or Trumaine he would be too big. He'd never ridden a racehorse before, but he could learn. Four years ago, he'd never ridden any kind of horse, and now he was pretty good at it. He thought of the electricity in the air before a race, the tension building while the horses gathered in the paddock, then headed out onto the track when the horn blew, tossing their heads, pulling at the bit, knowing it was time. The jockeys knew it too, but right then, cantering down to the starting gate, they relaxed a little bit, real light in the saddle, gathering all their energy for the race. And then they'd get their horses into the starting gate—some of them not wanting to go in at all, no matter how much practice they'd had. *They* knew this was something else. And then, they were off!

219

Thundering hooves. Blurs of color, and the announcer's voice—if you were in the stands—calling out the positions, while you strained to see. But if you were out there . . . If you were on one of those horses you'd see maybe the sweaty rump of the horse in front of you, you'd see tails whipping, glints of flashing shoes. . . . Or maybe you'd see a clean track in front of you. You'd hear the crowd roar and you'd be hitting the tape, gone away . . .

Flea whimpered and nudged his leg with her nose. "All right, Flea, in a minute." JoBob went down the aisle, topping up the water buckets with Flea padding along beside him. Then he closed up the barn for the night and Flea was off like a shot, running ahead of him on the path toward home. She knew where they were going, and JoBob bet she was pretty hungry. *He* was hungry, for the first time in a long time.

Hungry as he was, when he came to the edge of the woods, before he started on the path toward home, he stopped and looked back. The long rays of the lowering sun painted the whole scene rosy: the big oak tree in front of the barn, and the big barn, glowing like an ember, the fences of the corrals, the ring, the jumps. JoBob was washed over with the strangest feeling he'd ever had. Sad, like maybe he'd never see it again. All mixed up in that was another something—a lot lighter, which made him feel cheerful. And hopeful.

Flea came scampering back and yelped at him. "I don't know what it is yet," JoBob told her. "But it's something new. I think."

Flea frisked her tail with satisfaction, as if she *did*

220

know, and trotted back toward the path home. JoBob swung in behind her and thought, that was a Bright One. Like the opposite of a Dark One. Dark Ones made him shivery and scared, but Bright Ones . . . Well, he supposed he'd find out soon enough.

When he got home, he didn't bother to circle around and see if his father's truck was there or not. If it was, he was going into the house anyway. He was too tired and hungry to do anything else and coming in the back way would save a good five minutes.

When he came out of the woods, across the fields by the cockpit, he saw something that made him go weird all over: his father and Chet and four or five other guys walking around, talking. A couple of trucks were pulled up facing the pit, and when it got dark JoBob knew what would happen. They'd turn the lights on, so they could see, and they'd be working far into the night, getting everything ready for the fight next day.

The fight next day! He'd been waiting a long time for this. "Whooee, Flea," he said softly. "This has been some kind of day, all right."

Flea cocked her head quizzically, and JoBob said, "Now you be real quiet. I know you're hungry and tired. I am too. Won't be long now." He turned and headed back to the circle-around route. He didn't want to see his father just now. He had a way of picking up on things and JoBob was so keyed-up he might give something away. He was tempted to go call the sheriff right then, but that was silly. He'd wait until the next day. Until there were fifty, sixty guys out there, and more than a hundred cocks. *Then* he'd call. And they'd come. They'd round up the whole lot of them. Book them and throw them in jail, and hit Gavin with a lot more than the rest of them. It was against the law to be at a fight, to use gaffs, to even own fighting cocks. But to have a fight on your property and be making book would land you with more time and a bigger fine. He knew, because he'd heard his father and Chet talking about it enough times. His father always said, "Oh, don't be such an old maid, Chet. We're out in the toolies here. No fuzz is coming out here. Half the time folks we *invite* can't find the bloody place. And even if the law does show up, we've got it hidden pretty good."

They did have it hidden pretty good. But JoBob knew where it all was. He'd give the cops directions to the house and then he'd take them out the back way, where they'd surprise the hell out of everyone at the fight.

22
###

NEXT MORNING JoBob woke up early. It was another sizzling day and lying in bed with nothing on except his underpants, he was already dripping with sweat; and his stomach was churning worse than it ever had before he went into the ring on Blue. His mind was churning too, thinking about how he was going to get through the morning and what would happen after that. The fight wouldn't start until one or two o'clock. All morning, people would be arriving. They'd be doing all the prefight stuff, strolling around, taking a look at each other's birds, chewing the fat. JoBob wouldn't see this, though. If he went down to the pit, it might make his father suspicious, since he'd made so much noise about not going to another fight.

At one o'clock JoBob would go to town. He'd put a handkerchief over the telephone receiver and give the whole story to the sheriff. Now, how was he going to get to town? Wished he'd considered some of these details weeks ago when he had time to think. Okay, calm down, he told himself, you've still got hours. Hitching was too risky. He might not be able to get a ride. And his bicycle had been out of commission for months. The only vehicle on the place that ran was his father's truck and he had it down by the pit. On Sundays the bus didn't run. Maybe he could go to the barn, saddle up Choo-choo or Auburn and ride into town like the Lone Ranger. Come back with the band playing and . . . No, that was just plain silly. Neither one of those horses had ever been out on the highway. They'd spook at a car, or step on a bottle and get cut up. And what if he did get to town and the guys at the fight got wind of it somehow? So when the sheriff and his deputies got there everybody would have cleared out? Then they'd get *him* for false accusation or something. No, it would be better to call from here, he finally decided. If Mabel Tompkins heard and started blabbing it around, so much the better. Then another kind of crowd might arrive. Someone from the SPCA and the weekly paper. People who thought cockfights were disgusting and would be glad to see "Cockfighting Ring Brought to Justice."

Darlene had gone off with Parnell and his mother had gone to early service at church with Mrs. Myerson down the road. JoBob ate some cereal and read the funny papers: Dick Tracy, L'il Abner, Pogo, Flash Gordon, Buz Sawyer. Then his mother came home from church. She changed her clothes, and went out onto the back porch with a basketful of dirty laundry. The old wringer washer had a loose bearing or something—it made a terrible clanking noise and stank of burning oil while it was running. Wouldn't run much longer if somebody didn't fix it. She'd been after Gavin for months to fix it and he always said he'd get around to it soon.

JoBob went out onto the back porch. "Want me to fix this machine, Mom?" He already felt freed-up. He could have fixed the washer a long time ago, too, but it had never occurred to him. His father just being around put a damper on everything.

She looked up and said, "Well, now, that's sure a nice thought. Do you know how?"

"I think so. It's a pretty simple motor."

She changed the hose for the rinse cycle. "Oh— Never mind. I need that machine almost all day today and your father said he'd fix it. He'll do it tomorrow."

"Sure he will."

"Well, he said he would. Be easy as pie for *him*."

JoBob was hurt. His father was a lot better mechanic than he was, but his mother was so dumb, sometimes. Believing that Gavin would actually do what he said he would. And not believing that JoBob *could* do it.

"Tell you what," she said, almost as if she knew she'd hurt his feelings "If he doesn't fix it tomorrow, then you can do it. If I don't get these clothes washed today, we'll all be walking around naked next week."

"Okay," JoBob said. "You know where the manual is?"

"Take a look in our bedroom. Box in the closet is where he keeps most of that stuff."

JoBob went into their bedroom and pulled the orange crate out from the closet. Piles and piles of old magazines—*Popular Mechanics, Grit and Steel,* that idiotic cockfighting magazine his father loved so much, *The Saturday Evening Post,* newspapers so old they were yellow and cracked. The only manuals he could find were for a Model A and a '26 Packard. Well, that washing machine motor *was* pretty simple. He could do it without the manual. It would be a pleasure to work on it without his father standing over his shoulder telling him he wasn't doing it right.

He shoved the crate back into the closet and shut the door. From down by the pit he could hear a low buzz. In a few more hours it would crank up to more than a buzz. There would be yells of excitement, and squawks of fury from the cocks, and then . . .

He went into the front room and turned on the TV. Turned it off. Went into the kitchen and tried reading other parts of the paper. "Eisenhower Recuperating," the headlines said. "Adenauer and Dulles Discuss the Berlin Wall." "Stevenson Wins California Over Kefauver in a Landslide." "Will Ike Run Again?" It was all so remote. All those guys in Washington or Berlin, or wherever they were. What did they have to do with him? JoBob went up to his room. Came back downstairs again, waiting, waiting. He went into the front yard and pottered through some of the junk there. Went back into the house and had a glass of iced tea. Kitchen was the best place to be. He needed to be near the phone. It was fixed firmly to the wall, but he needed to keep his eye on it. It might go away if he wasn't holding it firmly in his vision.

The second hand crawled around the clock, but it did keep moving. Finally it was time. He stuck his

226

head out the back door to see where his mother was. She was hanging the wash on the line. Perfect. He pulled his handkerchief out of his back pocket and took the receiver off the hook. Good old Mabel Tompkins blabbing about her sciatica. Damn it, damn it, damn it. Trust her either to be talking on the phone or listening in. JoBob thought the receiver had probably grown into her ear like mistletoe into a tree.

For fifteen minutes he picked up the phone every few minutes, and every time she was still yakking. Every time he slammed the receiver back onto the hook and went back to pacing.

Finally he picked it up and spoke. "Uh, Mrs. Tompkins? Excuse me, but do you think you could get off the phone, please? It won't take long and it's a sort of an emergency."

"Well landsakes, JoBob, whatever is the matter? Nothing serious, I hope. Why, I saw your mother this morning in church. She said you were all fine. She tell you about the sermon? Pastor Gillette has such a beautiful voice and . . . You ought to have been there. Young people thinking they can get along without the Lord and . . ."

"No, no it's . . ."

"What do you mean 'no'?! The Lord forsaketh those who . . ."

"Just lay off!" JoBob yelled. "And let me use the phone. Couple of minutes is all I need. Hogging the phone isn't very neighborly or Christian, either!"

Mrs. Tompkins clucked indignantly. "You hear that, Lila? You hear what this child said to me? I never."

JoBob's cheeks were burning, but it worked. She

hung up. He wondered if she'd heard about casting the mote out of her own eye. But no, old bag like that interpreted the Bible according to her own convenience.

He jiggled the button to get the operator, glad that it was Bobbie Sue Moore, the weekend operator. She wasn't nearly such a busybody as Edna Nixon, the regular operator. He didn't bother with the handkerchief. Hadn't fooled Mrs. Tompkins for two seconds, so he doubted it would work on Bobbie Sue either. Probably one of those things they did in movies that worked in the movie, only because all sorts of things worked in movies that didn't work in real life.

"Get me the sheriff, please." JoBob said, making his voice as deep and grown-up as he could.

"One moment, please."

JoBob waited, tapping his foot, his stomach getting weirder and weirder.

Bobbie Sue came back on the line. "It's busy, sir. Shall I try again later?"

"Yes, please. Thank you." He hung up the phone, wishing that he'd gone to town, after all, where he could have used the phone booth at Patton's Service Station. A private line. Because if Bobbie Sue ever did get the sheriff, Mabel Tompkins would be on the line again, you could bet on that. Things were not working out the way they were supposed to.

"What are you doing?" his mother asked. Her voice shrill, scared. "Calling the *sheriff?*" JoBob jumped about two feet in the air. Things were *definitely* not working out according to plan. Well, she'd find out when the sheriff pulled up. Might as well know now.

"Yeah."

"Whatever for?"

"Reporting the fight. It's about time he paid for some of the sh—some of the things he's been doing."

"Call the law on your own father?"

"Yes! If Pop's in jail, he won't bother you anymore. Me either. It's about time he learned he can't go . . ."

"Don't do it, JoBob."

"Why not?"

"Because . . . because . . ." She sank into a chair and her hands dropped to her lap as if they were much too heavy for her arms to hold up. "Because I need him. It would break his spirit."

"*Need* him? For what? What good did he ever do you?"

"You're too young to understand. Maybe someday when you find the girl of your dreams and she . . . and she . . ." She stopped and choked. "And she turns out to be something different than what you thought, then maybe you'll understand."

"Are you talkin' about him being different, or you?"

"Oh, both of us, I suppose. Life has a way of handing out things you don't expect and you do things maybe you're not so proud of. You change. You grow. And not always in the same direction. The same way."

"If I wound up with somebody like him, I would leave."

"I would hope that you wouldn't. That you would have some Christian charity. Know that she needed you and you wouldn't leave her in the lurch."

"But it's against the law."

"Oh well . . . He's not hurtin' anybody. And it's

the one thing he really enjoys."

JoBob thought he was going to throw up. "He hurt *me!*"

"I know he did. And he shouldn't have done it. But I thought you were a bigger person. You're talkin' about doing the kind of thing *he* would do. Out of spite."

JoBob was still standing by the doorway to the front room where the telephone hung on the wall. All of a sudden his legs stopped holding him up and he sank to the floor. This was turning out to be a lot more complicated than he'd thought. He thought she'd be pleased to have him out of the way. Ever since the night he'd found out Blue was gone, when she'd taken JoBob's side, when she'd told Gavin he was wrong . . .

The phone rang then. One long and two shorts. Their ring.

"Mom?"

It rang again.

"You get it," she said quietly. "It's your decision."

JoBob was in turmoil. Here was the chance he'd been waiting for. The chance to get back at his father. To make him pay for selling Blue—and a lot of other things. Pictures and scenes were going through his mind real fast: his father when he was angry, his face dark, his eyes hard. Himself—JoBob—picking up a dead cock with its head flopping and the blood oozing, and flinging it onto the trash heap. The picture of his parents on their wedding day, his mother so young and pretty and hopeful, his father handsome as could be with his arm draped possessively over her shoulder.

Trumaine dancing at the Sacramento show, his eyes half-closed, singing, "A little love that slowly grows and grows . . ." And through it all, Blue. Blue's face, with the bright cheery blaze, hanging over his stall door in the morning, nickering hello to JoBob. His kind eyes. Blue trotting into the ring beside JoBob, tossing his head with pride. And Slim. The twinkle in his eyes when he was telling a story on himself. Mariko holding the hawk feathers. Then a voice that maybe he'd never heard, only imagined or read—"Vengeance is mine, saith the Lord." All this in only a few seconds; because when JoBob noticed where he really was, the telephone was still ringing. His mother was sitting at the kitchen table where she'd sat down a couple of hours ago, it seemed, looking not hopeful or sad or even defeated. Just resigned. The telephone rang again and JoBob stood up very slowly. He saw the telephone. An odd black object like something he'd never seen before. On the wall next to it, skittery cracks in the plaster.

Slowly, slowly his hand reached for the receiver. He picked it up. "Hello? No. Nobody here called the sheriff. Must be some mistake. Thanks, Bobbie Sue."

The faucet dripped in the sink, the Frigidaire hummed, out on the back porch Flea stirred and sighed. Then his mother's voice came low, sing-songy, almost as if she were talking to herself. "I thought about leaving, Lord knows I have. Hasn't been easy, you know it hasn't. Years ago, years and years, I thought about it and I nearly did it, but he . . ."

231

"Mom, you *can* leave. You're not so old. You can move to town, get a nice apartment, have a whole new life."

"No. I am too old. It's too late. I promised to stick by him for better or for worse, and that's what I'm going to do. Decided to do a long time ago. He's weak and he needs me. Understand?"

"I guess so."

She took a deep breath. "But it's not too late for you. You are young. And I know you'll make me proud. You already have." Tears were running down her cheeks, but she was smiling through the tears and her eyes were not sad.

"So you go on, Joby. I chose this life and I'll stick it through, but here's your chance. You go on down to L.A. and take that job at Hollywood Park. Why, maybe I'll be reading about you in the newspaper one of these days."

"I guess maybe I will."

"Wish you could have stayed and finished school . . ."

"Oh, school. I've been to school long enough."

"Seems like it *is* time for you to go."

They were quiet for a long time, then she started talking again, the same sing-songy voice. "Did I ever tell you about when I was a kid? I was a little younger than you. Twelve, thirteen—something like that. It was evening and I went out to the well for a bucket of water. One of those beautiful summer evenings back in Virginia when the air is soft as feathers and the little night sounds are all around. Things were stirring around inside me too—yearning kinds of things

232

I didn't have any name for—I reckon you know what I mean." She paused and her chest was heaving. Jo-Bob's was too. He'd never heard her talk like this. He never had any idea she knew about his yearnings, either. "I brought up the bucket from the well and set it down. I sat down, not wanting to go back into the house right away. Then I noticed the moon. The moon in that bucket of water. Prettiest thing I ever saw, all shimmering and silvery. Round and . . ." She smiled and her eyes were very faraway. "I didn't have many pretty things, or any other kind of thing, either, but I had that moon. I could take it home with me, and it would be a comfort—my very own moon. So I did. I went home with the bucket, all excited. I set the bucket down on the front porch, and looked into the water, and . . ." Her voice caught and JoBob thought she was going to cry again. She swallowed and smiled and he'd never seen her look sadder. Or sweeter. "The moon was gone."

JoBob wasn't sure what she meant. He didn't know what to say, either. He was overwhelmed. "I don't get it."

"Oh well, I didn't get it for a long time, you see. A long, long time. Means you can't *have* some things. But if you let go, let them be in their proper place, then they're yours in a way no one can take away. But first you have to let go. Like you just did. Let go of the hate and the hurt . . ."

She stopped and JoBob didn't move. He sat, letting it all sink into him, slowly. He thought he knew what she meant. He felt like he'd accomplished something very important. He felt grown-up, too. He'd never be as tall as his father and that was a good thing. If he were six feet tall he'd never be able to go to the track, gallop horses, be an exercise rider, maybe a jockey if he was good enough. Inside it was different. Inside he was a lot bigger. He knew it, even without his mother saying so.

Quiet, it was so quiet there in the kitchen. JoBob felt quiet inside too, for the first time since Blue had gone.

GODLEY MIDDLE SCHOOL LIBRARY